Now Playing

Black Panther

(A Novella)

DEDICATION

This book is dedicated to my grandchildren:
Benjamin, Avery, Nico & Remy

May the tribes of their world
be more tolerant of each other
than the tribes of my world.

Chapter One

Cinema Paranormal

The Strand Theater on Main Street in Enfield, Connecticut, was a quite ordinary brick and mortar, gummy-floored 20th century movie house. It was neither exceptionally ornate nor historic. The fire department was located across the street and a couple hundred steps down to the right on the banks of the town's Mill Pond. The police station was a few steps to the left, across from the old Congregational Church and the obligatory war memorial. There was nothing really extraordinary about the theater nor its setting, but then there was nothing really extraordinary about Ford's Theater in Washington, DC, until Abraham Lincoln was shot there and nothing extraordinary about the Biograph Theater in Chicago until the FBI tracked gangster John Dillinger down there and shot him outside. Fate occasionally intervenes and renders the ordinary extraordinary.

Shep Farrell was just putting the *K* in place to finish the word *Black* on the Strand marquee when his boss, Leo D'Aleo, stepped out and looked up to check his work. "Hey, Shep," Leo yelled to the young man at the top of the ladder, "You spelled *Creature* wrong."

Shep leaned back on the ladder as much as he dared to read the signage he'd spent the last hour working on: *The Creture from the Black...*

"I did?" he yelled back down.

"Needs an *A* after the *E*," Leo yelled back up.

"Damn. I'm a terrible speller."

"Don't curse it, Shep. Just fix it. I'm heading over to the post office to pick up the film now. Then I'll drive by the house and get Rosemary. You'll have plenty of time to screen it and then help her get the lobby ready for the first showing."

The first showing of the weekend's new double feature would start off with *Creature from the Black Lagoon* at 5. Shep was always excited about Friday night openers, which usually brought out a good sprinkling of Enfield's young people. Although the theater couldn't get a 3-D copy of Creature, the national publicity surrounding it seemed to Shep to make it a cinch Friday night date ticket, even at 50 cents for those 16 and up.

Enfield in 1954 was a monochromatic town. Most of the recent

European immigrant families who had settled there--even the Sicilians--muted their native colors to better blend in with the staid descendants of the town's original colonial settlers. With no color TVs, the only time hue and saturation mattered at all was when one of the new Technicolor films arrived in town. Such a film was *Carmen Jones*, which would be second billed on the double feature with *Creature from the Black Lagoon*. That might normally set *Carmen Jones* up for a bigger reception, but its Technicolor glory would be overshadowed by its all-black cast. In Enfield at the time there were as many blacks...or Coloreds, as they were called...as color TVs. No, the bigger draw for the upcoming weekend would not be the dazzling sights and sounds of the musical *Carmen Jones*, but the terrifying black and white thrills and chills of *Creature from the Black Lagoon*.

When Leo D'Aleo returned with his cans of film and daughter Rosemary, he was happy to see *Creature* spelled correctly and happy to see *Carmen Jones* on the marquee in smaller-sized letters. He and Rosemary entered the Strand to find Shep sweeping the lobby. Rosemary scuttled over to kiss Shep on the cheek, and Leo winced at the thought that he might soon have a son-in-law who could not correctly spell the word creature...and so many other words. Then the three of them gathered over the candy counter as Leo opened the heavy cardboard box that contained a trio of canned reels of the new film. Each can featured a strip of masking tape upon which someone had hand-written the title: *Creature from the Black Lagoon.* Leo slid the box over to Shep. "There you go. Load it up."

"Roger," said Shep, the Strand's projectionist as well as its sign maker, floor sweeper, and usher. "Do you want me to call you when it's ready for screening? I think it's going to be cool."

"Got enough scary stuff in my real life. I don't need to look for it in the movies." With that, Leo picked up the last of his mail and headed up to his office on the second floor.

"What did he mean by that?" Shep asked Rosemary, who was watching after her dad with obvious concern.

"I don't know," she answered, stepping behind the counter and starting to shelve boxes of candy.

"Well, I think this one's going to be a hit. Come up to the projection booth when you get a minute, and we'll do some smooching and screaming together." She smiled wanly as Shep put the box of film under his arm and headed upstairs to the projection booth.

Shep's sausage-like fingers were serious obstacles in his training to be a projectionist. The delicate task of sliding the film through the camera's sockets and then looping it around to the pick-up reel was not meant for someone with blacksmith's hands. Days of lots of trial and error on the arduous learning curve almost convinced Leo D'Aleo not to hire the then 18-year old Shep. And if Shep couldn't handle the projectionist's job, Leo couldn't afford him to be the theater's Jack-of-all-trades either. More pressingly, Shep was Rosemary's boyfriend of two years already, and Leo had promised her he'd hire him full-time after high school graduation. So Shep became the Strand's projectionist, though he'd never win any ribbons at the job and even though his hands still shook and he broke into a sweat every time he had to thread a film. As excited as he was about *Creature from the Black Lagoon*, it was no exception. As soon as he unfurled enough film to slide it into the camera sockets, he started sweating.

But this time something inexplicably amazing happened. As soon as he brought the edge of the film close to the sprockets, it threaded itself...like a trained seal looping itself through a pool full of inner tubes...and when it slipped ever so smoothly around the pick-up reel, it came to a stop at exactly the point a professional projectionist would've stopped it. Shep had to step back and look on it in total astonishment. Then he gingerly moved his index finger toward the off/on switch and flicked it up, allowing just enough playing time to see that it worked right...but not enough time for the color that briefly flashed on the screen to register with him as anything other than a ghostly shadow.

In the theater manager's office, Leo was staring glumly at a piece of mail that had arrived with the *Creature from the Black Lagoon* when his daughter walked in.

"Pop," she said, "we're out of Good & Plenty and have less than a box of Juicy Fruit and Milk Duds. What's happened to the inventory?"

Leo pushed the problem piece of mail toward Rosemary. She picked it up and read it. "Foreclosure notice!" she exclaimed. "But how?"

"How, Rosemary? Jack Benny is how. Jimmy Durante. Ed Sullivan. Tonight...Friday night boxing. All on TV. For free. People don't want to leave their living rooms and pay for entertainment any more. The movie business is dying. We're dinosaurs. The Strand is a dinosaur."

Rosemary flung her arms back and raced to embrace her father, "Oh, Dad...Dad, this is awful. What are we going to do?"

"I've been wrestling with this for six months, dear. I'm out of ideas."

"Does Mom know?"

"It's why she asked for extra hours at the hospital even though she hates the night shift."

Just then there was a strange, loud noise and the office shook.

"What the hell was that?" asked Leo, jumping out of Rosemary's arms and his seat.

"An earthquake?" guessed Rosemary, reaching for him.

"In Connecticut?"

Shep burst into the office with a look of perplexed wonder on his face. "Quick. You've got to come see this."

Leo and Rosemary hurriedly followed him out the door and down into the auditorium. When they all got there, they came to a stop in the aisle at the last row of seats and stared up at the screen. On it, a forbidding-looking, bald-headed, tattooed black woman in shining red leotard and holding a spear smiled wickedly. There was another black woman...young and exotic...who approached a huddled group of black women dressed in desert garb and told them they were free to return home. But before they could leave, the woman with the spear warned them not to tell anyone what they just had just seen.

"All these Coloreds," Leo said. "Is this *Carmen Jones*?"

"I don't know," said Shep. "It was labeled *Creature from the Black Lagoon*, but when I turned it on there was a meteor crashing to earth and then animation of all this fighting going on in Africa and then it cut to some live action involving Colored hoods in Oakland, California...in 1992. That's when I ran to get you."

"Look at all this color and listen to that sound," said Rosemary in awe as a rocket soared through majestic cliffs and waterfalls.

"Look at all these Negroes. It must be *Carmen Jones*. You must have put the wrong reel on," said Leo. Then he did a double take at the screen and said, "Wait a damn minute! Did that Colored girl just give that Colored boy *the finger*?"

"I think she did," Rosemary confirmed.

"Jesus Christ," said Leo, "The Legion of Decency is going to be all over us if they ever see that. Go shut this goddamned thing off," he ordered Shep.

As Shep ran off to do as he was told, Leo shook his head at the screen, "All these Negroes and no singing. No dancing. Who would want to see such a thing?"

No sooner were the words out of his mouth than the movie switched to a heist scene at a British museum, allowing Leo to briefly get his bearings. "Wait a minute. Now it's like *Asphalt Jungle*. But in color. With white people." As the heist scene unfolded, Leo struggled to find comfort in the familiar genre. But before he could, the film switched back to a futuristic landscape as pulsating African music filled the theater and hundreds of dark-skinned people in vividly multicolored dress filled the screen, standing in cascading formation on sheer soaring bluffs and flanked by roaring waterfalls.

"I've never seen anything like this," marveled Rosemary, in wide-eyed wonderment.

Shep reappeared and sheepishly confessed, "I can't get the projection room door open."

Leo looked at him with mounting impatience. "Oh, for the love of…" He trudged off to the projection booth. Shep and Rosemary exchanged worrisome glances, took a passing glance at the elaborate tribal ritual unfolding on the screen, and then marched on off after Leo. At the projection booth, Leo struggled with the doorknob, but couldn't get the door to budge. "Did you lock it?" he demanded of Shep.

"No. It must've locked by itself."

Leo shook his head in disbelief, and then dug into his jacket pocket for the theater keys. He quickly identified the projection booth key, jammed it into the keyhole and turned it. Another shove at the door yielded nothing. He turned on Shep. "Help me here, dammit."

Shep joined Leo at the door and together they thrust their shoulders into it. Then again. And again. "Jesus H. Christ," muttered Leo.

"Do you want me to go to the fire department for help?" asked Rosemary.

Leo looked at her warily. The idea of opening this predicament up to outsiders was unappealing. Then he stepped away from the door and looked down at his movie screen where two muscular black men were engaged in the most ferocious fight he'd ever seen in a movie as an all too realistic, thunderous waterfall threatened to engulf them and the entire auditorium. This movie playing in his theater was too enormous and lifelike to be just a movie. Something seemed to be happening that was beyond him, and he really did need help. He turned back to Rosemary and said, "Yes, but only Cap Kelly. I don't want the entire department in here seeing this."

By the time Rosemary returned with fire chief Cap Kelly from a few doors down, the *this* on the screen had become an eruption of car chase noise and violence. Kelly was immediately dumbstruck by what he saw on the screen and joined the others in muted disbelief as screeching, big, black, futuristic vehicles careened over an urban landscape from another world. High-powered guns a-blazing onscreen turned the theater into a war zone. When one of the vehicles did a terrifying flip into the air, the awestruck audience of four ducked as one to the floor. "What the hell?" yelled Kelly. "What in the five-alarm hell?"

Leo signaled Kelly to follow him, and Rosemary and Shep joined them as all four, careful to keep their heads down, made their way to the projection booth. "What's going on here?" asked Kelly, once they reached the projection booth door.

"No idea," said Leo.

"It's supposed to be *Creature from the Black Lagoon*," said Shep.

"We can't get into the projection booth to turn it off," added Rosemary.

Kelly looked around at all three of them to absorb their collective discombobulation. Then he made a try in vain at the door. "You got the key?"

Leo held the key up to him. "Already tried it," he said.

Kelly took the key from him, put it in the door, turned it and tried again in vain to open the door. In exasperation, he turned to Leo and asked, "What do you want me to do? Take an axe to it?"

"We've got to put a show on for an audience at 5. I've got to get control of my theater back," Leo lamented.

Kelly rubbed his hand up and down the door and then looked Leo straight in the eye. "So's it worth a new door to you?"

"Has to be," Leo replied. "Do what you have to do."

When Kelly returned with his axe, the others were watching intently as another fight over the waterfall between two muscular black men unfolded on the screen. Kelly was instantly intrigued and suggested to Leo that he just let the movie run to the end and see what happens. Rosemary and Shep both endorsed the idea, but Leo was adamant. "The end? How do we know when this movie will end or if it even has one? How do we know where it's going to go from here? We're sitting on a time bomb with this thing. I don't trust it. I don't like what it's doing. We have to stop it. Now. Break the damn door down."

With that, Kelly lifted his axe and took a hearty swing at the door. The door rejected the axe, and the shock wave from the hit nearly knocked Kelly to the ground. "Holy shit!" he exclaimed. "It's not a wooden door?"

Shep ran his hand over the door. "It's wood alright," he proclaimed, before jumping out of the way of Kelly's second swing. The door's resistance bounced the axe out of Kelly's hands and sent it flying dangerously close to Rosemary's head.

"This goddamn movie!" Leo yelled out of alarm for his daughter's life.

"I don't know what in Jesus name you've got going on here, Leo," said Kelly, humbled. "But that door's not coming down with an axe, and it seems that movie's going to run 'til it gets to the end. You better make plans accordingly."

"Plans?" said Leo defiantly. "I'll show you a plan." He turned to Shep and ordered him to go to the main power panel and turn off the electricity. Then Leo, Rosemary, and Kelly watched as Shep made his way down to a side door to the right of the screen. He disappeared into the darkness there, opened the panel and flipped the switch. The movie kept playing.

"Turn it off," Leo yelled.

Shep stepped out of the darkness and yelled back, "It's off."

"Goddamn it," Leo exclaimed, still clinging to the belief that his problems were due to Shep's incompetence. He ran down to the side door himself. He pushed Shep out of the way, opened the panel cover and flipped the switch: *On...Off...On...Off.* He ducked his head out and looked up at the screen where the movie was still playing. He went back inside and flipped the switch one more time for good measure, but still the movie rolled on. Leo looked up at it with mounting hostility and then stormed up the aisle, passing his daughter and the fire chief. "Someone's going to hear about this," he vowed.

As Shep joined Rosemary and Kelly, they shared a shrug of bewilderment with one another and then took seats in the auditorium to watch the movie.

In his office, Leo put in an angry call to Epstein Brothers, his film suppliers from New York. Izzy Epstein took the call and 30 seconds into Leo's complaint told him he was drunk. "I'm not drunk. Come on up here and look at this thing you sent me. It's taken over my movie theater!"

"If you're not drunk, you're crazy. We sent out 35 copies of *Creature from the Black Lagoon* this week. You're the only one to call and complain it's taken over your theater. You should get your head examined."

Leo slammed the phone down on Izzy's ear, got up and headed for his car. As he drove 10 minutes up over the state line to Springfield, Massachusetts, Rosemary, Shep, and Cap Kelly let the bizarreness of the circumstance go and settled in to enjoy the latter part of the big, colorful, action-packed movie playing out before their bedazzled eyes.

In Springfield, Leo parked outside the Bijou and hurried inside to find Barry Grossman, its manager. An usher directed him into the auditorium where Barry was standing at the back watching the closing minutes of a black and white movie. Without prolog, Leo demanded to know what Barry was watching. "*Creature from the Black Lagoon*," replied Barry. "Aren't you showing it this weekend?

"You got it from the Epstein Brothers?"

"This morning, like always. Didn't get yours?"

"They sent the wrong movie."

"Too bad. It's going to be good business."

As Leo's shoulders slumped and he turned to exit, Barry called after him, "Show the one they sent you. Epstein can't charge you for it, and the audience won't care. A movie's a movie."

Back at the Strand, Leo had to confront just that option. People were already lining up for the 5 o' clock show. As he entered the theater, he passed Cap Kelly walking out muttering, "Never saw anything like that. Never."

Inside the lobby he was greeted by Rosemary and Shep and asked, "Any change?"

"It ended," Rosemary said.

"Thank you, Jesus, Mary and Joseph," said Leo prayerfully.

"And then it started all over again," Shep added.

"Just like that?"

"Ten minutes later."

"Without a reel change?"

"All on one reel."

"What do you want to do about the line outside, Dad? Those are paying customers."

"But here to pay to see *Creature from the Black Lagoon*, not a bunch of half naked Coloreds flying through space and shooting up white people…and that Negro girl giving the finger. The Church can shut us down just for showing that."

"We can't shut it down," said Shep. "It's just going to keep on playing. Who knows how long?"

"If you're not going to let people in to see it," Rosemary argued, "you may just have to lock the doors until it stops."

Leo looked at her with relief and then dug into his pockets for his keys. "That's it. We'll lock the doors and let it play itself out." He headed for the main entrance, opened the door, and yelled down the ticket line, "Sorry, folks, the distributor sent the wrong movie. No *Creature from the Black Lagoon*. Sorry…sorry. Another time. We'll let you know."

As moans and groans rose up from the crowd, Cap Kelly and four of his firemen showed up from behind Leo. "Leo," Cap Kelly bellowed, "Gotta give the boys a glimpse of this thing. Damnedest movie I've ever seen…" With that, half the Enfield fire department marched into the lobby and made its way to the auditorium with Leo,

Rosemary, and Shep in quick pursuit.

"You can't," yelled Leo, "We're shutting the theater until further notice. No show tonight." But by the time he got the last words out of his mouth, the firemen were swept up in the strange and remarkable images flickering over the movie screen and were settling into their seats for more.

Moreover, out on the street the chief's declaration about "the damndest movie" he'd ever seen quickly passed through the crowd and was translated into "the grandest movie" he'd ever seen, and people poured into the theater. Within a few hours the movie that Shep and Rosemary had watched through the end credits would begin capturing the imagination of the entire town of Enfield, Connecticut, and begin spreading panic all the way to the nation's capital.

Rosemary cast a sympathetic look down on her forlorn father and whispered in his ear, "It's called *Black Panther*."

Chapter Two

The Spirit of Yorba Linda

Coincidently, while the residents of Enfield were undergoing a science fiction-like experience watching a movie called Black Panther, the science fiction film they were originally meant to see, *Creature from the Black Lagoon*, had just finished a private screening in the home library of Richard M. Nixon, Vice President of the United States. Nixon's loyal wife Pat sat in an armchair across from him as the final credits rolled and he rose to turn the lights up.

"Did you like it, Dick?" she asked tentatively.

"Like it, Pat?" he stated, retaking his seat. "This isn't a damn film appreciation exercise. This is Ike's future I'm in charge of here."

Pat picked up the unpublished manuscript on the end table by her elbow, realizing that the opportunity to discuss with her husband a film that they'd just spent an evening at home watching had passed and that Dick Nixon was now in the role he relished most –grand inquisitor.

Dick looked at the publicity shot that accompanied *Creature from the Black Lagoon*—a buxom beauty in a tight, white bathing suit being carried off by a horrible beast whose left claw comes dangerously close to clutching her left breast. As salacious as it seemed, he knew he'd be accused of making a mountain out of molehill if he tried to sound an alarm about it. It was really nothing more than a thinly veiled facsimile of the famous poster from *King Kong* of the ape carrying off Fay Wray. The clear implication of bestiality aside, the nation was unlikely to be aroused to outrage by an image it'd been comfortably living with since Betty Crocker first appeared on a box of pancake mix.

He then looked over at the stack of recent Hollywood films piled on his coffee table that he'd spent the last few weeks watching and studying--*Rear Window, Dial M for Murder, The Caine Mutiny, The Garden of Evil*. He'd been searching for depravity gold, but despite the promising titles, none of the films offered the transgressive immorality he'd been hoping to find. He had a lot invested in this search. He'd convinced his boss, President Dwight David Eisenhower, that they could counter the comic book investigation of

Ike's possible 1956 challenger, Estes Kefauver, by pinning an alleged decline in American morals on the movies. The Tennessee Democrat Kefauver, like the Wisconsin Republican Joe McCarthy, had blazed a new trail in forging a top tier political identity through riveting, televised congressional hearings. Americans, just getting accustomed to televisions moving in and taking over their homes, seemed to welcome open combat with open arms whether it was live Friday night boxing matches or live daytime political skirmishing. Through their respective televised hearings both Kefauver and McCarthy were gaining a notoriety previously reserved only for those at the top of the political pecking order. And those at the top were taking notice, especially Eisenhower, who didn't beat Hitler by taking him lightly. Plus Ike felt he had nothing to lose if Nixon wanted to spend his free evenings watching movies in hopes of coming up with something fresh and outrageous enough to pivot off the blacklisting of Hollywood reds and reduce Kefauver's comic book gambit to child's play.

But Nixon was coming up empty...murder, mutiny, manipulation. None of it was going to hit home with the impact of Kefauver's dire warning about the nation's children being turned into juvenile delinquents through comic books. On his end table Nixon had a copy of the transcripts from Kefauver's hearings. He had flagged numerous pages and underlined copious passages to inspire him in his task of coming up with a trump card to Kefauver's pioneering work. As he thumbed through it once again, his eyes fell on the passage he'd come back to again and again. Kefauver's star witness, Dr. Frederic Wertham, a consulting psychiatrist with the New York City department of hospitals, was giving testimony and said this according to the transcript:

I would like to point out to you one other crime comic book, which we have found to be particularly injurious to the ethical development of children and those are the Superman comic books. They arouse in children phantasies of sadistic joy in seeing other people punished over and over again while you yourself remain immune. We have called it the Superman complex.

In these comic books the crime is always real and the Superman's triumph over good is unreal. Moreover, these books like any other, teach complete contempt of the police....

All this to my mind has an effect, but it has a further effect and that was very well expressed by one of my research associates who was a teacher and studied the subject and she said, "Formerly the child wanted to be like daddy or mommy. Now they skip you, they bypass you. They want to be like Superman, not like the hard working, prosaic father and mother."

Nixon marveled at that...the ability to twist a benign figure...indeed, a heroic figure...like Superman...and turn him into a villain...a threat to family and home. He understood instinctively how that could stir much deeper emotions than could such an abstract concept as communism. He knew the only way you could really ratchet up feelings against communism was to call it godless...to warn people that under communism their churches would be closed and they wouldn't be allowed to pray in their homes.

Nixon, however, didn't really trust religion as a tool to achieve political ends. He believed most people were—like him—only cosmetically religious for the sake of putting their best faces forward. Culture, on the other hand, was deeper and could stir darker impulses. Kids tried to hide their comics...sneak into movie theaters; no one tried to sneak into church, hide their Bible. Yes, he was intrigued with the idea of using culture to foment passions and bend political will. So he read on:

In many comic books the whole point is - that evil triumphs; that you can commit a perfect crime. I can give you so many examples that I would take all your time.

I will give you only one or two. Here is a little 10-year-old girl who killed her father, brought it about that her mother was electrocuted. She winks at you because she is triumphant.

I have stories where a man spies on his wife and in the last picture you see him when he pours the poison in the sink, very proud because he succeeded.

There are stories where the police captain kills his wife and has an innocent man tortured into confessing in a police station and again is triumphant in the end.

I want to make it particularly clear that there are whole comic books in which every single story ends with the triumph of evil, with a perfect crime unpunished and actually glorified.

In connection with the ethical confusion that these crime comic books cause, I would like to show you this picture, which has the comic book philosophy in the slogan at the beginning, "Friendship is for Suckers! Loyalty—that is for Jerks."

That passage always caused Nixon to pause and ponder. He agreed completely with Wertham's observation that the bad guys...and the so-called anti-heroes...were gaining in glory...were getting away with more and more thanks to depictions of their roguish charm and secret smirks. He saw that in spades among his political enemies and the press...the way they cackled behind his back. But it was Wertham's last declaration there about friendship being for suckers and loyalty for jerks that caused Nixon complex second thoughts. He wasn't sure if he didn't half agree with it. The half being that if he was honest with himself—and on this he was—he kind of believed that friendship and loyalty ran just one way. And he wasn't going to be a sucker or jerk for anybody. So screw friendship and loyalty. He puffed up at that, feeling just a bit of a rogue himself at that moment.

"How many times are you going to read that transcript?" Pat asked, intruding on his self-esteem.

He looked down at the page in his hands and said, "Listen to this." Then he proceeded to read to her more of Wertham's testimony:

If it were my task, Mr. Chairman, to teach children delinquency, to tell them how to rape and seduce girls, how to hurt people, how to break into stores, how to cheat, how to forge, how to do any known crime, if it were my task to teach that, I would have to enlist the crime comic book industry.

Formerly, to impair the morals of a minor was a punishable offense. It has now become a mass industry. I will say that every crime of delinquency is described in detail and that if you teach somebody the technique of something you, of course, seduce him into it.

Nobody would believe that you teach a boy homosexuality without introducing him to it. The same thing with crime.

"Think of it, Pat," he said looking directly into her eyes. "Comic books turning all American kids into criminals and queers right under their parents' eyes. If I can't come up with a way to counter this, and Kefauver can sell it to the country, Ike's re-election hopes will go up in smoke no matter how many Nazis he defeated."

Pat looked back at him, sensing the presence of his ambitions, delusions, and resentments—the trio of not-so-secret mistresses in their marriage. She looked back down at her own reading.

He knew in an instant he was losing her. "What have you got there," he asked with the same conjured up, feigned interest he had used to get through college, their courting period, and his congressional career.

"This?" she said, holding forth the unbound manuscript pages she was reading and knowing that he'd just given her a cue to play the happily married couple. "It's a book Anne Lindbergh is writing. She's calling it *Gift from the Sea*. She gave it to Mamie to read, and Mamie asked me for my opinion."

"Typical Eisenhower. Because Mamie doesn't want to take a chance on not liking it and insulting the Lindberghs. So she's going to leave it to you to do her dirty work for her."

Pat's eyes fell upon one of Anne Morrow Lindbergh's observations on the page in front of her: "*When you love someone, you do not love them all the time.*" She sighed.

"Boy, that Lindbergh," Nixon said, barreling through her sigh. "Crossing the Jews. First rule of American politics: Don't cross the kikes. He could've been president, but now they'd never let him."

He waited for a response from her with nervous sweat beginning to form on his upper lip, his five o'clock shadow beginning to darken, and his ski jump of a nose beginning to ice over from the falling temperature in the room. But he couldn't help himself. "Do me a favor," he said, "Don't let the Jews in the press know you're reading that thing. They're not dragging me down with goddamn Lindbergh."

Chapter Three

Never on Sunday!

In the time it took Richard Nixon to conclude that he couldn't forge a
winning campaign strategy for Ike around a prehistoric creature
from a black lagoon, the 134 minutes of *Black Panther* had captured
the full, frenzied attention of the parochial little town of Enfield,
Connecticut. Word of the film's majestic audio and visual qualities
had spread rapidly through the town, first through its younger
population. But by late Saturday afternoon its round the clock
showing had begun to attract older folks…parents, teachers, police,
the board of selectmen…even Barry Grossman had deigned to travel
from Springfield to Enfield to check it out. "I want that fucking
movie," he told Leo as soon as he'd watched it. "How do I get it?
Where? Who? Tell me. I want it. You gotta give it to me as soon as
you're done with it. Helluva movie. Hell…hell…helluva movie!"

Leo had to give up trying to stop people from flooding through the glass doors of the Strand for the oldest of reasons: there was too much money to be made. His biggest problem turned out not to be the black girl in the film flashing "the finger", but finding enough help to sell tickets and popcorn. For that he enticed his wife Ellie to give up the night shift at the hospital to pitch in. He also found willing volunteers to work the concession stand in exchange for a chance to stand at the back of the theater and watch the film again. At the rate the money was coming in he stood to take in as much from this rogue film over the weekend than he had for all the featured films of the past six months.

By Saturday night, *Black Panther* was all anyone could talk about. Televisions went dark all over town as people sat around their living rooms telling each other what they had seen…the mesmerizing hand-to-hand combat; the spectacular battle scenes; the exotic weapons; the car chase that seemed to jump off the screen; the taut, muscular bodies…clothed and unclothed; the taut, muscular *black* bodies. The people of Enfield had not seen so many *black* bodies since *Gone with the Wind* had come to town serving up a screen full of slaves.

Those who weren't sitting at home talking about it gathered across the street from the Strand talking about the film they had just seen or hoped to see or hoped to see again. As the audience emerged from each successive showing, the milling crowd would pull them in for questioning...looking to confirm their own recollections of what they had seen. Crowd control became an issue in Enfield for the first time in its history, but an easily resolved issue since there was no shortage of police and firemen signing up for the duty.

Though their community had been totally upended by the appearance of this mysterious cinematic force, the townspeople seemed quite willing to give into it. Not a word of complaint or objection was uttered...until Sunday morning. That's when Father Francis O' Boyle looked out on his flock for the first Mass of the day and found it consisted of Mary Barton, 78; Nellie Bridges, 82; and Gina Mangini, 64 and blind. His yoked trio of altar boys hadn't even shown up. He hurried through the liturgy as if he had diarrhea, quickly threw together some communion wafers and wine for the ladies, and was so quickly out the door in search of the rest of his flock that he didn't even bother to pass the collection basket.

It didn't take long to find his parishioners...the Strand was located at the other end of Main Street from St. Pat's, and from his church he could see his flock with what he quickly determined was a false god before them. He broke into a run for the theater. When he reached the crowd, he found it in a festive mood. Though it made no sense to him, many had painted themselves in blackface and were shouting lines from the movie at each other:

Fat boy in blackface: "If you say one more word, I'll feed you to my children."

Skinny boy in blackface: "He's kidding. We're vegetarians."

Mr. Blair, social studies teacher in blackface: "Is this Wakanda?"

Miss Brooks, girls' gym coach in blackface: "No, it's Connecticut!"

Mr. Blair: "You would kill me, my love?"

Miss Brooks: "For Wakanda? Without question."

Fat boy and skinny boy in unison: "Wakanda forever!

"Have you seen this picture yet, Father?" Cap Kelly asked from behind his blackface.

"I have to see Leo D'Aleo about this," O'Boyle declared, marching toward the theater.

"Damndest picture you ever saw, Father!" Kelly shouted after him.

In Enfield in 1954 priestly garb could get you through most any door without paying a price, and so it was that Fr. O'Boyle didn't even feign at buying a ticket. He burst through the glass doors and sought out Leo D'Aleo amidst the hubbub inside. "Leo, Leo," he shouted, as Leo collected tickets at a madding pace. Show times were now dictated by an inanimate film projector that allowed no wasted time between seatings.

"Go right in, Father," Leo shouted back, ushering the priest to the auditorium door.

"I'm not here to see a movie," yelled O'Boyle. "We need to talk."

"Sit anywhere," said Leo, trying to bluff his way past a talk he didn't have time for.

O' Boyle looked around in total bewilderment as the crowd pushed all around him. Shep brushed by him with boxes of Mint Juleps for restocking the concession stand. "You gotta see this one, Father," he said to the man in black. "It's better than *The Robe*." Then he caught himself, looked apologetically at O' Boyle, and said, "Forgive me, Father."

O' Boyle did not so much walk into the auditorium as he was sucked in by the crush of the crowd. He fell into an aisle seat in the last row, and like everyone else who'd bowed before that screen in the past couple of days, he was awed by the power and glory of Black Panther's light and shadows. But unlike all those others, he refused to surrender totally and wholly to it, calling on his rigid religiosity to resist. So when he saw that Negro girl *give the finger*, it was not lost in the blur of story-telling magic. It was duly noted. And when another character said "shit", O'Boyle bowed his head and prayed. And when heaven was portrayed as a place full of primitive black tribesmen and jungle animals, the priest reaffirmed his determination to discuss with Leo D'Aleo exactly what unorthodoxy was unfolding in his movie theater. As much as he wanted to witness what further blasphemy the movie would offer up, the priest believed that he had to seize the moment to speak with Leo. "*Carpe diem*," he muttered to himself, rising up from his seat and rushing into the lobby. There he found the still frazzled but less busy theater manager assessing the crowd outside his doors. "Leo, we must talk," insisted the priest coming up from behind him.

When Leo turned around to face him, O'Boyle was stunned to see how ravaged he looked in the calm of the moment. "We're in over our heads here," D'Aleo said, clutching the cleric by his arm and guiding him up to his office...as Shep and Rosemary counted the most recent box office and concession receipts into bank bags.

In the Strand's inner sanctum, the priest took immediate control of the conversation. "Leo," he said, "You have to stop running this film.

It's corrupting the town. Church attendance today was in mortal sin territory...for the entire town."

Leo looked around almost helplessly, until his eyes fell upon a bank bag full of money. He picked it up and placed it in front of O'Boyle. "Here," he said. "For the collection plate."

O'Boyle took the bag in his hand and marveled at the heft of it.

"We've never made so much money," Leo told him. "I don't like it any more than you do, but I can't stop it from running. We've tried everything. It's out of our control."

The priest leaned back in shock. "You can't stop it?"

"Physically. We can't do anything to shut it down or off. It's like some kind of possessed demon."

"Possessed demon. Exactly!" exclaimed O'Boyle. "Well, lock your doors then at least. Stop people from seeing it."

Leo laughed a borderline psychotic laugh. "We tried. The doors won't lock." He threw his set of keys across the desk toward the priest. "Try it yourself. Bless them in holy water and try it yourself if you don't believe me."

The priest took up the keys and studied them. "I must report this to the archdiocese. The Legion of Decency will have something to say about this. "

Chapter Four

La Casa Blanca

A limousine dropped Richard Nixon off at the South Portico of the White House and he rushed to the West Wing to make a Sunday lunch meeting in the Oval Office. When he entered, the other participants were already in the room munching on liverwurst...and even though he was technically 5 minutes early he immediately became sheepish. Senator Prescott Bush of Connecticut was on the phone standing at the President's desk and was first to acknowledge him with a wave *hello*. As he approached the others gathered in chairs around the fireplace, each greeted him in turn thusly:

President Eisenhower: "Dick."

Secretary of State, John Foster Dulles: "Dick."

John Foster Dulles's brother Allen, Director of the Central Intelligence Agency: "Dick."

 Texas oilman and son of Sen. Bush, George H.W. Bush: "Dick."

Nixon quickly calculated the alliances: two Dulleses, two Bushes, and Ike, neither kin nor kind, so he was alone on an island again. *Screw you, John Donne*, he thought to himself...and not for the first time. The President nodded toward the couch, indicating that Nixon should have a seat. As Nixon carefully chose a corner to settle into, Prescott Bush finished his phone call and strode across the room, holding a hand out to Nixon, "Dick."

Nixon grabbed at the hand like a lifeline.

"What was that call about?" asked Allen Dulles, always with his antenna up.

"Odd bit of news from back home," the senior Bush replied. "Some movie theater in the north end of the state is running the same film over and over again around the clock and it's causing quite a hubbub."

"Crazy Connecticut," chuckled the younger Bush. "Sounds like they're getting bored watching the grass grow."

The others joined young Bush in laughing, except for Nixon who silently begrudged the rich, athletic Yalie for the easy bonhomie he was able to strike up with his fellow elites.

"Shouldn't laugh, son," advised the elder Bush. "Some day you may learn that these are the kind of problems public servants live for."

More laughter, save Nixon, busily stewing over the fact that young Bush wasn't even part of the government...had never won an election.

"Your young fella's already served the voters," John Foster Dulles told Prescott Bush. "In Operation AJAX, George's contacts in the oil industry and willingness to act behind the scenes helped us put the Shah of Iran back into power and kick the communists out."

"Not just Iran," added John's brother, the spook, "What you did to help bring about a change in regime in Iran helped provide the blueprint for our current efforts in Guatemala. So, yes, yes, indeed, thank you, George."

"Hear, hear," Eisenhower chimed in. "George has become quite the secret agent."

"My son, James Bond," added Prescott Bush, provoking mild laughter around the room, again except from Nixon.

"Let's not laugh," said John Foster Dulles. "George could have Allen's job one day."

"Ha! That's a good one, Mr. Secretary," laughed George, "but tell me the secret of how we managed this coup in Guatemala. Some day I might want to take over Texaco."

Another burst of laughter, and this time Nixon did join in. He liked the idea of George H.W. Bush taking over Texaco and keeping his damn snot-filled nose out of politics.

"Well, of course you can always ask your tennis buddies from United Fruit about that," said Ike, "but if you want to hear it from the horse's mouth, we have the horse right here. Tell him, Allen," the President commanded.

"Ahh, *Operation PBSUCCESS*," the chief spook began, peering directly at George over his glasses. "You begin with destabilization. We got out the word that there was a revolution brewing...that this so-called democratically elected government couldn't hold, that it wasn't as popular as people thought. Get them second-guessing their own votes. Then we started planting stories in the press about the new government's ties to communist secret arms purchases and so forth."

"And boots on the ground, don't forget boots on the ground," added Eisenhower, forever the soldier. "Don't make out like this is all a lot of psychological hocus-pocus. Ultimately you need men marching through the mud with guns to pull this kind of thing off."

"The President is right of course," acknowledged Allen. "Guns on the ground and guns in the air. We bombed the hell out of their oil reserves."

"That finished off Árbenz...not our guy," added the diplomatic Dulles, "and then a few chess moves later we had installed Armas...our guy."

George H.W. Bush fell back in his seat, clapping his hands, "Howdy! You guys are good."

"They left out the part where one of Allen's agents left the plans in his Guatemala hotel room. They were published in the papers for most of the world to read, but you may not have gotten those papers in West Texas." It was Nixon speaking, although he may very well have been emitting a big, deep liverwurst-infused burp for the effect it had on the room.

"Dick," said Eisenhower, breaking the icy silence. "Tell us. How's your movie watching going?"

"Dick's watching movies?" questioned Prescott. "I thought you were all about high culture, Dick. Didn't I hear you tinkling on the piano once?"

More laughter at Nixon's expense spread through the room.

"Dick has this idea that if we can expose the movies as morally corrupting we can cut the legs out from under Kefauver and his comic book crusade."

"That sounds pretty damn strategic," commented young George Bush, with a note of insincerity.

"Diabolical," added John Foster Dulles.

"Maybe we can use some old Eisenstein films to bring down Khrushchev," added Allen Dulles to haughty chuckles.

On that high note—for most—the Oval Office meeting broke up. The Dulles brothers took their leave first, identically bidding adieu: "Mr. President. Senator. George. Dick."

The Bushes then shook the President's hand, thanked him for his time, and passed on to the Veep. Prescott patted Nixon's shoulder and said, "We have this film up my way everyone's going mad about, Dick. Maybe I can get you a pass."

The younger Bush was more ebullient in parting from Nixon, vigorously shaking his hand and saying, "Next time I'm in town we'll have to have a drink so you can tell me *all* about the Vice Presidency."

Nixon, who believed he had scored the winning point in that one-on-one, was suddenly dejected as he watched the elitist son of a bitch do a touchdown dance out the door.

"Dick," said Ike, intruding on Nixon's self-loathing, "Don't leave. I have something for you."

Nixon followed his boss to his desk and dutifully filled the seat numerous underlings had occupied. Eisenhower took the seat that Nixon secretly lusted for. "I need you to do something important for us. Take the lead on these upcoming congressional races. Goddamn Joe McCarthy is taking the entire party down with him and we can't allow that. I want you to travel around the country...show that we stand with our candidates. Give speeches. Raise money. Whatever the hell else it takes."

Nixon struggled up from his impending gloom. "Begging your pardon, Mr. President, but couldn't we get Mamie and Pat to do that? I can lend my girls. I think my talents would be better used elsewhere. There must be another Iran or Guatemala we want to overthrow. Hell, give me a shot at China."

"How about if I send you up to Connecticut to investigate this runaway movie Prescott's talking about?"

Nixon cast the President a bewildered look.

"Just kidding," Ike said charitably. "No let's leave it to the Dulles boys to take care of the big bad world outside. I need you in the Great Plains; New England; your home turf, California. Can I count on you?"

Nixon sat there looking like the last man in the world the Commander-in-Chief could ever count on.

"Dick…Dick…Dick…"

Chapter Five

Sin City

Though there had been rumors and fears that no one in Enfield would go to work or school on Monday...that, as on Sunday, the entire town would crowd in or around the Strand...it did not happen. Quite the opposite, in fact. People were so much excited to share their experiences watching or hearing about *Black Panther* that they flocked to familiar work and school settings in record numbers to commune with each other. Even employers and educators welcomed the heightened chatter because the spirit that attended it was so rare and energizing.

At the local Bigelow-Sanford carpet mill, supervisors joined workers on cigarette breaks and shared their favorite scenes:

"That car chase...you ever see anything like that?"

"Never saw cars like that."

"And that rocket flying through that canyon? Forget Flash Gordon. I got dizzy just watching it."

"I liked the waterfall fight."

"Which one?"

"Yeah, which one?"

"Both. It was like something in a Tarzan movie, only ten times better."

"And when those rhinos showed up. How'd they do that? I didn't see any strings or anything. How'd they do that?"

"Two guys in a rhino suit, I'd guess."

"Go on!"

The kids at Enfield High were into all that and more as they gathered in pockets around lockers and buses:

"Shuri, the sister character, was funny. I like how she always gives it to her brother ."

"Yeah, she is cool."

"And how about those shoes she invented?"

"And that suit...that suit...that was the best...way better than Superman's."

"How about Batman?"

"Way better. But Catwoman. Now we're talkin'. Man, those Colored girls in those tight suits. You could practically see everything."

"Yeah, forget *National Geographic*...that was just plain graphic."

"Graphic as all hell. I'd see it again just for those girls in those suits."

"I have sin dreams about those girls in those suits. And I ain't talkin' venial sins neither."

Little did any of them know that their chances of seeing it again hung in the balance as a long black limousine pulled up in front the Strand. As a chauffeur came around to open a rear door, Father O'Boyle scurried out to take a place at the rear of the car. Then both black-clad men stood solemnly as Archbishop Henry O'Brien stepped out. He sniffed the air around him and looked back at the crowd gathered across the street from the theater. It was smaller than the Sunday crowd and less boisterous. Like the crowd inside the theater at that very moment, it was somewhat older, more representative of Enfield's senior and retired citizens with a sprinkling of folks from the mill's night shift. The maturity level produced a respectful hush in honor of the visiting cleric who followed O'Boyle into the theater.

The lobby did not present the madhouse that greeted O'Boyle on his first visit, which both calmed and dismayed the priest. Although he didn't want to lead his superior into the chaos he encountered 24 hours earlier, he did want there to be a scene to warrant the urgency he invoked to call O'Brien up from the Hartford Archdiocese.

"A matinee crowd it seems," said the Archbishop, indicating that he was underwhelmed by O'Boyle's alarm.

"It's the film, your Excellency," said O'Boyle in mild dread; then quickly turned to Rosemary behind the counter, "Rosemary. The Archbishop is here. We need to see your father."

Rosemary cast a hurried look up at the clock and then a panicky look at the two clergymen standing in the middle of the lobby. She rushed to them and pushed them both against the wall featuring posters of the now obsolete double feature: *The Creature from the Black Lagoon* and *Carmen Jones*. No sooner had she gotten them out of harm's way than the four big auditorium doors flew open and the crowd from inside poured out. Random comments reflected the more sober assessment of the film by the older crowd.

"That was very noisy," said one elderly woman.

"I can't hear you," said her companion.

"All that killing and crashing around," said another. "I don't like so much killing."

"I never saw so many Coloreds in one place in my whole life," claimed an old man. "I don't like it."

"Women Negroes with guns and spears. Punching and kicking. Where will it lead?" asked another. "And those outfits. Very vulgar."

Rosemary held the holy men against the wall, protecting them until most of the crowd filed out. Then Leo, Ellie, and Shep came through the doors, each pushing a wheelchair-bound patient. Ellie, in her nurse's uniform, was the first to see the trio at the wall. "Father O'Boyle!" she hollered with a smile, leading the wheelchair caravan on a detour over to Rosemary and the Catholic clergy. There were introductions and greetings all around, which is when the religious professionals learned that some of the patients from the hospital where Ellie worked were bussed in to see the movie, and the theater staff learned that Father O'Boyle had called the Archbishop in to investigate *Black Panther*. With that sobering news, Ellie, Shep, and Rosemary pushed the wheelchairs out to their waiting transport, while Leo led O'Brien and O'Boyle into the auditorium to secure prime seats before the next showing. O'Brien asked for a Tootsie Roll, and O'Boyle went and fetched it for him. Leo excused himself to man the box office.

Soon O'Boyle and O'Brien were surrounded by another full house, most of it baptized and confirmed Catholic, near jubilation in anticipation of the movie it was about to see. With the dreaded scene of Shuri lifting her middle finger to her brother, O' Boyle felt such embarrassment at having invited the Archbishop to witness this profanity that he wanted to drop to the sticky floor and hide under his gummy seat. Instead he sat there awash in guilt as O'Brien watched all 2 hours and 15 minutes of the movie totally inert.

Shep stood at the back and watched most of it himself again, except for a brief visit to the concession stand to see if Rosemary needed help. "How many times have you watched that now?" she asked him.

"I've lost track," he replied.

"And you're not tired of it?"

"Just the opposite. I'm awakened by it."

"Shep Farrell, listen to you talking like a poet. I'm *awakened* by it."

"It's true. I never had a movie open my eyes like this. Not just to the sights and sounds, but the message. It has a deep message I think."

"And what do you think that message is?"

"It's about Colored people...how they're treated. Slaves and all."

"Oh, *pshaw*, slaves. There haven't been slaves in a hundred years. You don't know anything about Colored people."

"I knew Paul Robeson when he lived over on Enfield Street."

"That opera singer? You *knew* him?"

"He used to give free concerts to raise money for the Enfield Teachers Association Child Welfare Fund. My mom was one of the organizers. She took me backstage a couple of times to meet him."

"I didn't know that about you. He was practically the only Negro who ever lived here."

"And his family," Shep added. "His son went to Enfield High."

"What was he like?"

"The son?"

"No. Paul Robeson. You're the only person I know that actually knows a famous person. Tell me about him."

"Well, he was a lot more like the Colored guys in this *Black Panther* movie than he was like Steppin' Fetchit or Amos 'n Andy. He was tall and powerful looking with this rich, deep voice. And, I don't know, dignified I guess. Just the way he carried himself...like this T'Challa character...proud like."

"But wasn't he a communist?"

"I guess, but you listen to Killmonger and you begin to wonder."

"Killmonger?"

"The bad guy in the movie...Erik Killmonger."

"Gosh almighty, Shep. You know all their names? I think you've watched that thing too much. Time to take a break. We all need a break..." and then she interrupted herself. "Uh-oh," she said as the auditorium doors burst open and the audience emptied out.

The Archbishop and his priest made a beeline for the theater manager's office. "Your holiness, this has to be quick," Leo said in greeting as they walked in. "I have to help with the next wave."

"The waves have to stop," O'Brien told him. "You can't keep showing this film. What's the count?" he asked O'Boyle.

O'Boyle pulled out a small pad and read from it: "One extremely vulgar gesture...two swear words...I think...ahm...."

"Nipples," declared O'Brien, cutting O'Boyle off. "Female nipples. The screen is full of them."

"But they're Colored girls," Leo protested.

"They're obscene," O'Brien countered. "The Legion of Decency won't stand for it. Do you remember your oath?" O'Brien cast a sharp, commanding look at O'Boyle who immediately recited the oath: "*I condemn all indecent and immoral motion pictures, and those which glorify crime or criminals. I promise to do all that I can to strengthen public opinion against the production of indecent and immoral films, and to unite with all who protest against them. I acknowledge my obligation to form a right conscience about pictures that are dangerous to my moral life. I pledge myself to remain away from them. I promise, further, to stay away altogether from places of amusement, which show them as a matter of policy.*

"*Places of amusement*, Mr. D'Aleo," repeated O'Brien, underscoring the point once O'Boyle finished. "This theater...*your* theater. You know what I think, Mr. D'Aleo? I think the devil has taken over your theater. The devil trying to strike back at the Church for Fátima, where the Virgin appeared and which has now been sanctified by his Holy Father in Rome. Satan has turned the Strand into his own perversion of Fátima. Those images on your movie screen are satanic apparitions."

"Dad," said Rosemary, popping her head through his door. "All hell's breaking loose."

"Figure of speech," Leo assured the clerics. "I'll be right there," he told his daughter. Then he looked around his office in befuddlement until his eyes landed on the sacks of money in the corner. He picked one up and handed it to Archbishop O'Brien, who at that moment was placing an expensive fur and felt black fedora on his head.

"What's this?" asked the startled celibate.

"A donation to the Archdiocese," said Leo, heading out the door.

As they watched Leo exit, O'Brien turned to O'Boyle and said solemnly, "This may call for an exorcist."

Chapter Six

Gentlemen's Agreement

Threats come to America in colors. Between the Yellow Peril of 1875 and the Black Panther Panic of 1954, there were the Red and Lavender scares that climaxed on June 8, 1954. That was the day Senator Lester Hunt, Democrat of Wyoming, committed suicide in his senate office. Hunt--one of the last of the now extinct species, a Wyoming liberal Democrat--was part of a bloc that tried to put some restraints on red-baiting Republican Senator Joe McCarthy. Hunt and his allies proposed a law that would restrict congressional immunity by permitting private citizens to sue members of Congress for making slanderous statements against them.

However, in June 1953 Hunt's son Buddy was arrested on morals charges for soliciting sex from an undercover cop. McCarthy and his Senatorial henchmen went to Lester Hunt and demanded that he resign his Senate seat, which would allow the Republican governor of Wyoming to fill it with a McCarthy ally. If he refused, they threatened a widespread smear campaign against him and his son over the arrest. Hunt refused, and after his son was convicted and fined in October of 1953, Hunt announced he was running for re-election. But the McCarthyites were unyielding and again threatened Hunt, leading to his suicide.

It was against this background that President Dwight David Eisenhower sat at his desk in the Oval Office looking over the results of the 1954 midterm elections. The feeling he had, he thought, was similar to the feeling his German enemy generals must have had after the Allies' *Operation Dragoon* sent their army skittering out of Southern France. Except in this case it was his Republican Party that was on the run. It had lost control of both houses of Congress to a revivified Democratic Party, which had withstood attacks by Richard Nixon to paint it as soft on reds. And even the so-called lavender scaremongering of homosexuals failed as Lester Hunt's replacement retained his seat for the Democrats.

The President's secretary knocked, entered and announced that Senator Prescott Bush had arrived for their meeting. "Send him in," said Ike, soberly.

"Mr. President," said the sunny Bush, striding confidently across the room.

"Senator," said Ike, motioning to a seat on the other side of his desk. He scooped up the election results and waved them halfheartedly at his guest. "The voters didn't much like Ike yesterday, Prescott."

"Ebb and flow, sir. Don't take it personally. It wasn't you they rejected."

"You mean you don't think they took too kindly to my Vice President's strategy to portray the opposition party as communistic with all this nasty McCarthy business in attendance? You'd think Lester Hunt's suicide would've given him pause before embarking on such a reckless and disreputable strategy." Ike continued, "Dick's thinking seems to be that the only thing wrong with McCarthyism is McCarthy; Dick thinks, 'Let me show you how it's done.'"

"They're eulogizing Lester in the Senate today...even Welker and Bridges, who tormented him. 'A man who demonstrated the best qualities of an American,' one of them said."

"They have no shame," said Ike.

"But they were right on one thing. Lester Hunt was a good man," added Bush.

"A good man caught in a damnable business. It cost him his life, and it's costing our party its reputation...and maybe its future. Prescott, something's got to be done about McCarthy. We have to move as a party against this menace or McCarthyism is going to eat us alive."

"I agree, Mr. President. I--and possibly others--are preparing to speak out against him on the Senate floor."

"It's got to be more than a goddamn speech, Prescott. I can't be head of a party with Joe McCarthy rotting out its core."

The two men shared a quiet, contemplative moment, before Bush spoke again. "We can try for a censure vote, Mr. President."

"It can't be just a try, Prescott. It's got to be a kill. If you try and fail, you'll turn him into a martyr and his power will only increase after that. You've got to succeed."

"We'll do it, Mr. President. I promise." Bush, sensing that the President had gotten what he wanted out of the meeting, got up from his seat. Then he stopped and said, "One more thing, Mr. President. If I may?"

"What is it, Prescott?"

"Do you remember that odd business I mentioned to you last time I was here about the movie that keeps playing over and over again?"

"Wasn't that a month ago?"

"It's still playing. Around the clock, and I'm afraid it may be coming a bit of a social unrest issue."

"How so?"

"Well the theater is located in Enfield on the Massachusetts border. Big immigrant population, but mostly white if you view the Italians as such. This movie has an almost entirely Colored cast…"

"Like *Carmen Jones*?"

"Yes. Like *Carmen Jones*, but no singing or dancing."

"What the hell is it then?"

"It's like Flash Gordon or Buck Rogers…"

"With Colored spacemen?"

"Why yes."

"I'll be damned."

"I don't know how much they believe it, but lots sure do like it. They've been showing up at this little movie theater, the Strand, nonstop to watch it morning, noon, and night. There are people in that theater at 3 in the morning watching it. It's taken down Sunday morning church attendance, Wednesday night bingo, and Saturday afternoon bocce ball. Bocce's big in Thompsonville."

"Thompsonville?"

"Enfield. Same place pretty much. Though it's looking less and less the same with every passing day. This movie...it's called *Black Panther*...has a very strong pro-Negro message, and it's beginning to draw Negro crowds from Springfield and Boston. New York even, I hear. And that's making the natives a little nervous. They thought they had this movie all to themselves and took some civic pride in it. It's really pretty amazing..."

"You've seen it?"

"Some of the local business and civic leaders reached out to me to come take a look. I've really never seen anything like it...surely no movie."

"What? Is it one of these 3-D things? I don't much care for those. Don't like wearing the glasses."

"No. This is beyond 3-D. This is really beyond anything, and now I'm afraid it may be generating one of those racial situations. And you know how those go."

"Jesus Christ. Don't tell me that. What's happening?"

"Well, as I say, the locals were all right sharing the movie with outsiders when it was just whites, but now that they see cars, trucks and busses of Negroes caravanning in to see it, they're getting a little testy. Some shoving back and forth in the movie queue…a bus got rocked back and forth. Some fruit got thrown. Small scale stuff right now, but it could escalate."

"Czechoslovakia."

"Huh?"

"Come on, Mr. Yale man. Czechoslovakia…small scale stuff started WWII."

"Right."

"What do you want me to do about this?"

"The governor's getting a little shaky and is talking about calling up the National Guard to surround the theater and keep anyone from watching it."

"The National Guard! Good God. Why doesn't he just set a cross on fire in the town square?"

"But no one knows how to stop this movie from playing. They've tried everything. They can't turn it off. I asked the theater manager what his plan was. He said they're waiting for the projector bulb to burn out. Who know when that will happen and how long tempers hold? And you know Negroes."

"A race riot on top of everything else. Over a goddamn movie, no less. We can't have that, Prescott."

"No, we can't. I thought maybe if you could send someone from the Army Corps of Engineers to look things over. Maybe there are airwaves or magnetic fields or something causing this. I think we should get on top of it...or at least give a show of getting on top."

The President pushed himself away from his desk and walked around behind his chair, and took a long thoughtful moment with his back to Bush. Then he turned and said, "All right. You'll get some of our technology boys. And I'll send Nixon along with them. That'll make it high profile and maybe keep him out of trouble for a while."

"Thank you, Mr. President."

"Space Negroes," muttered Eisenhower. "What will they think of next?"

Chapter Seven

When a Stranger Calls

Richard M. Nixon's visit to Enfield, Connecticut--in the company of Majors Hicks and Briscoe from the Army Corps of Engineers--was indeed a big deal. It was accompanied by a parade through the center of town, which included delegations from the Veterans of Foreign Wars, the Rotary and Lions Clubs, the Enfield High School marching band as well as the Clippers and Clipperettes, a co-ed drill team dressed in sailor uniforms...the girls twirled batons, the boys twirled make-believe rifles. Though the town went all out, Nixon took his assignment as a personal slight and rebuke of all the hard work he'd put in watching movies. It was a painful reminder of his recent trips across country from New Hampshire to New Mexico, campaigning for Republican candidates he privately referred to as Congressman Nobody and Senator Simpleton.

When he emerged from his limousine with his ersatz wave and smile, he was met by the town's First Selectman and an executive from the Bigelow-Sanford carpet mill, who presented him with a checkered burgundy carpet swatch. Because he was traveling without his wife and because Hicks and Briscoe were immediately sundered off to survey the area and because his secret service attachment was under strict instructions to keep their hands free for emergencies, Nixon had no one to hand the carpet swatch off to after it was given to him. He looked at it helplessly as the official welcome dragged on, and then he carried it with him when he was led into the Strand. Inside the lobby, he was greeted by Leo, who was suffering under great ambivalence over this visit. On the one hand it had brought him unimaginable publicity for his small town movie house; on the other hand, this sudden attention from Washington where movies had become the proxy target in America's war with communism was very unsettling. In the few quiet moments Leo had been able to grab for himself since the madness had begun, he saw himself hurtling pell-mell--*Creature from the Black Lagoon* to *Black Panther* to government blacklist. Shaking Richard Nixon's cold, animatronic hand there in the lobby was not at all reassuring.

"Tell me about this movie problem," Nixon said, leaving pleasantries aside.

"Well, we can't seem to turn it off, Mr. Vice President," Leo told him. "It just keeps playing around the clock," Then pointing to the crowd gathered outside, he added, "And audiences keep showing up."

Nixon perused the crowd through the large glass doors, and said, "Yes, I understand that Negroes in particular are showing up."

Leo nervously looked over the crowd himself and though it was dominated by the town's white faces, who had shown up this day primarily for Nixon, there were still more black faces out there than one would normally see in Thompsonville in all of a year. "Yes," he said to Nixon. "They seem to like it a lot."

The First Selectman, who had been standing quietly aside, added without solicitation, "We really don't have the facilities here for so many outsiders."

Just then Ellie came by with her arms loaded down with dozens of empty popcorn boxes for the concession stand. Leo immediately grasped for her as a straw in the wind of his discomfort. "Ellie, please come meet Vice President Nixon. Mister Vice President, my wife Ellie." Ellie rolled her eyes at Leo as Nixon appraised her load.

"You're selling a lot of popcorn," Nixon remarked, though it hit Leo's ear as an accusation.

"Well, when we can," Leo said. "The audience usually rushes right in to grab seats because the movie just rolls on its own schedule. Some people come out for popcorn and candy during the slow moments, but there aren't many of those, so it's a problem all around."

Nixon held his carpet swatch out to Ellie and said, "Can you hold this for me?"

Ellie just turned and proceeded on to the concession stand without even answering, leaving Leo to feel even more awkward. "I can take that for you, sir," he said to Nixon.

Nixon looked down at the swatch in his hand to appraise it once last time for any hidden value and then perfunctorily handed it to Leo. "Let's see this damn movie," he said.

"Just about to start," said Leo, looking at his watch, feeling relieved to have the visit over but trepidation at what might follow.

At the concession stand, Ellie, Rosemary and Shep watched Leo and the dignitaries go through the auditorium doors. "Nothing good is going to come of this," warned Ellie. "I don't see how Nixon watches that movie without turning it into some sort of crisis."

Indeed. It took Nixon less than five minutes to get to red alert while watching *Black Panther*. As soon as the scene turned to two black men in an Oakland apartment with a cache of high-grade military arms discussing an attack of some kind, Nixon was in full crisis mode. The fact that the scene was set in 1992 did nothing to allay his fears...in fact it heightened them as he viewed the scenario as predictive...dangerously predictive. The scene framed his entire view of the rest of the film and totally skewed his perspective when it returned to the discussion of black, armed rebellion against worldwide oppression. Those moments reaffirmed his original impression that *Black Panther* was an incitement of Negroes despite the fact that the Black Panther character--the film's "good guy"-- argued against violence.

Without taking any written notes or tape recording of the overall message of the film, Nixon walked out of the theater with only his first impression: it was about angry Negroes with guns. "We have to put a stop to this thing," he told the First Selectman, as he charged out of the auditorium. When he confronted Leo in the lobby on his way out, he told him, "You have a problem here, Mister."

Outside he waded through the crowd gathered for the next showing, scowling. Because most Americans knew him by his scowl, it did not dampen their spirits and they shouted out to him:

"How'd you like the movie, Dick?"

"Where's Pat?"

"How's Ike?"

"Bomb Wakanda!"

When he got to the limousine, he was joined by Hicks and Briscoe. "All right, fellas, what's going on here?"

"Nothing unusual far as we can tell," answered Hicks.

"At least not on the surface," added Briscoe. "We'll have to conduct some tests back at the lab, but it all looks pretty ordinary."

"Ordinary? Shit. A film calling for Negro rebellion is playing nonstop and no one can shut it down?" fumed Nixon. He ordered his driver to get him back to Washington.

Inside the theater, the First Selectman told Leo what Nixon had told him: "We're going to cordon off the theater, Leo. I'm calling an emergency meeting of the town council and asking for funds to pay our police overtime to keep the crowds away until we hear back from Washington. Nixon wasn't happy with what he saw up on that screen. And frankly neither am I."

"But you've seen it five times," Leo protested.

"I *analyzed* it five times, Leo. That's what leaders do. I don't jump to conclusions." And with that he walked out of the theater and signaled the police detail to rope off the Strand.

"Doesn't jump to conclusions," mocked Shep, coming to Leo's side. "He sure enough jumped out of his seat when that big black wagon flipped and nearly jumped off the screen. Five times he jumped."

Ellie and Rosemary joined their men and all looked out on the police rope now circling the Strand. Rosemary sighed, "Looks like the show is over."

Chapter Eight

The White Panther

The police rope around the Strand theater was an unusual sight in Thompsonville. In the past, the most common use for the rope was to block off any holes that developed in the ice on Mill Pond across the street. As such, the populace was duly intimidated, and people who had been rushing into the theater in waves during the previous weeks of *Black Panther* fever now started treading cautiously. Rather than merely walk around the perimeter of the rope line, most everyone preferred to walk on the opposite side of the street on the sidewalk along the pond. This trepidation meant that the extra police the town council provided for were hardly necessary. Three cops on rotating 8-hour shifts seemed to do the trick.

Milo Dundee, who was the youngest of the cops and newest to the force of course drew the graveyard shift. On the second night of his watch, Shep, who had been dropping by the theater periodically to check to see if *Black Panther* was still running, brought Milo a box of popcorn as a courtesy. Milo, who said he was "bananas for popcorn", was grateful, but the conversation went swiftly downhill after that. Shep asked him what he thought of the movie, and Milo told him he hadn't seen it. And Shep expressed surprise because he thought everyone in town had seen it at least once. Then Milo surprised him even more by saying, "I don't want to see a movie with a bunch of niggers in it."

Shep stepped back as if Milo had hit him all at once with a blast of bad breath, a whiff of underarm odor and a juicy, wet fart. "Holy cows, Milo. It's only a movie. No one's asking you to marry one."

"They're dumb and lazy and sex crazy," Milo retorted.

"Jeezum," said Shep in surprise, "where'd you get all that information? We have so few of them around here."

"My father. He knows all about them."

"Well, maybe the movie will give you a different view."

"You think my father's a liar?"

"I don't know your father."

"You don't know niggers either. You watched a movie and now you think you're goddamn Abraham Lincoln."

Shep shrugged and said, "Enjoy your popcorn." And then he walked away. As he walked past an alley between two of the shops on Main Street, he heard a "Pssst...pssst" from out of the dark. He looked to his right and saw two people looking back at him. When he looked closer he could just barely make out that one was a tall black man and the other was a white woman.

"Shep," said the woman, "Can we talk?"

Shep cautiously stepped into the alley and the two beckoned him to follow. They went down the alley to the empty lot behind the Main Street buildings where a faint light illuminated all their faces and Shep was shocked to recognize the woman as Sheila Dundee, one of his former teachers and Milo's mom. "Mrs. Dundee!" he gasped.

She turned to the black man standing over her and introduced Shep to him. "Shep, this is Marcus Barber, a friend of mine."

Marcus put an arm around Sheila and pulled her close and said, "A dear friend." Then he reached out a hand to shake Shep's.

As Shep tentatively took the offered hand he looked at Sheila who smiled demurely. "We sat next to each other watching *Black Panther*," she said, "And then we had a coffee after."

"And then more coffee and more coffee," added Marcus. "Sheila likes it black." They both laughed, and Shep suddenly felt discomfort.

"I've left my husband," Sheila said, which did absolutely nothing to becalm Shep. "And I've joined the underground."

"What underground?" asked Shep, beginning to feel as if he'd walked into a Hitchcock movie.

"The *Black Panther* underground," answered Marcus. "We want to see that movie and we're not going to let any police cordon stop us."

"But you said you've already seen it," said Shep, relieved to suddenly be talking about the movie rather than adultery.

"Yes, we have," said Marcus, "But they haven't." And with that he raised a hand and gave an *olly olly oxen free* signal. And just like that from out behind trees and trucks and trashcans emerged an army of dozens of folks, which as best as Shep could decipher in the dark were all Colored people. "We got all these folks from the darker precincts who want to see this movie, Shep...who have a right to see it. We need your help."

Before Shep could plead helplessness, Sheila jumped in. "We overheard your conversation with that bigot son of mine, Shep. His kind's what's going to deny these people their right to see *Black Panther*. You've seen it. You know how powerful it is. This police blockade is only the beginning. They're going to find a way to shut it down completely so no one--Colored or white—will ever be able to see it. Before they do, we need to help as many people see it as possible."

"But how?" asked Shep, alarmed at the very prospect of getting involved.

"We want you to get us all into your theater, Shep," said Marcus. "Underground railroad style."

Shep looked beyond Sheila and Marcus to the throng of Negroes standing silent in the dark. This was a moment he could never ever have imagined for himself...where he--a white boy from Thompsonville, Connecticut--would have the hopes and dreams of so many Negroes riding on him. As he pondered his decision, he was quite certain that before viewing *Black Panther* numerous times, he would've turned his back and walked away from the moment. But the movie had clearly touched and changed something in him. Not that he was ever a Milo Dundee-level bigot, but his interactions with the Colored race had been limited to his few brief encounters with Paul Robeson, as he had described them to Rosemary. But the recent weeks of viewing *Black Panther* over and over again had helped him reach a comfort level with negritude he found good and liberating. The film had given identity and meaning to a race of people that had been largely anonymous and pawn-like to him, however benign. He began to reflect on many of the heroic movies he had seen in his humble role as projectionist at the Strand over the years... *High Noon*, *Shane*...just that summer *On the Waterfront*. He remembered the sense of exhilaration he got from them...of being infused with the idea of heroism...of wanting to do something heroic himself someday. "Get me on my feet," he said quietly to himself, channeling Brando's Terry Malloy from *On the Waterfront*.

"What?" asked Marcus.

"Am I on my feet?" he answered, more to himself than Marcus.

Marcus stepped back a bit, afraid Shep was losing it. "Yeah, you're on your feet."

Sheila took Shep by the arm and shook him gently, "You okay, Shep?"

"Yeah," said Shep, snapping out of his cinematic revelry. "Follow me." And he waved to the ebony-on-ebony assemblage, which stealthily fell in behind him as he led it through the hidden byways of Thompsonville to the unguarded back door of the Strand theater. He unlocked it for them, opened the door and they filed in to fill the empty seats...all perfectly timed as the closing credits of the previous showing filled the screen as prolog to the next full showing.

Marcus came up and put an arm around him. "Hey, man," he said in lowered voice to Shep's ear, "You're the White Panther now."

Chapter Nine

All the President's Manly Men

When Nixon left Thompsonville after viewing *Black Panther*, he felt as if he may have stumbled upon something useful for his own career as well as his Party's future and Ike's re-election. He smelled redemption from their disastrous congressional losses that November.

Who knew how much Kefauver's attention-grabbing show hearings into comic books had contributed to the Republican defeat. In 1952 Kefauver had ridden his televised hearings into organized crime into a run for the Democratic Party nomination for President. It was pretty clear that his recent pubic hearings into the connection between comic books and juvenile delinquency had elevated his public profile even more and set him up as a dangerous alternative to Ike. Nixon actually admired the gambit. McCarthy had pretty much cornered the market on scary communism and given red-baiting--Nixon's forte--a bad name. So the idea of beating up on some aspect of popular culture in order to convince the masses that they were under attack and needed a white knight to save them still had enormous appeal to someone with Richard M. Nixon's ambitions. *Black Panther* had breathed new life into his dream of trumping Kefauver's crusade against comic books and ingratiating himself to Ike with a crusade all of his own. With enough massaging, he believed he could use *Black Panther* to ring an alarm. It was with that purpose in mind that he prepared his report for Ike on his trip to Thompsonville and requested that FBI Director J. Edgar Hoover be present.

When they met in the Oval Office, Allen Dulles was also there. Nixon launched into what was intended to appear as an extemporaneous report, but had in fact been rehearsed to the last syllable:

"Mr. President," he began. "Director Dulles. Director Hoover. On my recent trip to Enfield, Connecticut, I encountered the most alarming motion picture I have seen in my entire life. Its name is *Black Panther,* and make no mistake, gentlemen, it's more black than panther and by black I mean Colored...Negro. The film is wall-to-wall Negroes...Negro actors playing Negro characters. Hundreds of them. Maybe thousands. There are only three white characters of any note in the entire film. One is a female museum curator who is poisoned by a female Negro. One is supposed to be a villain of South African nationality who is killed by a male Negro. The last is a rogue CIA agent and...you'll like this, Allen....he joins the Negroes fighting against other Negroes. There's a lot of that. From beginning to end it's Negroes versus Negroes. The savagery is nonstop. They're shooting each other, throwing spears at each other...kicking and screaming. I'm afraid it's a spectacle of all we've come to observe and expect from that race. With some sex thrown in there, of course. The females, all Negroes, are dressed in skintight outfits showing off every hill and valley of their anatomies. Most of them have those baldheads that we hear a lot about in Africa, so it's quite alien and disturbing, especially to see them killing with a fierceness that, I tell you, chills the blood. It sure did mine. It pretends to be science fiction, a Colored's version of Flash Gordon you might say, with all the tight outfits, the flashing weapons, rocket ships, what have you. But I believe there is something far more dangerous at work in this motion picture. I believe it has a corrupting intent, and it could most definitely serve as an incitement to actual civic unrest here in the United States. In reflecting on it during my ride home from Connecticut I thought long and hard about the Tulsa Race Riot of 1921. You all remember it I'm sure. But let me tell you how this

Black Panther motion picture stokes the embers of that uprising. The picture mostly takes place in an African kingdom called Wakanda…it's made up I believe…but, Allen, you can double check me on that. But I think someone's trying to sneak something by us. This Wakanda is a lot like Greenwood, where the Tulsa riots took place. It's an enclave of better off than you'd expect Negroes, living well off the professions…law and medicine and such…and oil that was discovered nearby. The Wakandans have got it pretty good too and have little to do with whites. To me it all seems inspired by that Marcus Garvey 'Back to Africa' nonsense…and Director Hoover can attest to what a pain in the ass Garvey was. Put the Negro race in a land of its own without white supervision and it will flourish. As if natural born cotton-pickers could ever pull a carat of diamond out of the earth without the white race showing how. It appears to me as if Garvey directed this motion picture from the grave, and it might be worth digging into more of his speeches and writing as we investigate further. Lots of fraud there, as I recall. And the other Negro leaders, like W.E.B. DuBois, didn't like Garvey. You get a lot of that in *Black Panther*…warring factions. The tribalism we see wherever these people breed. Of course it was the young bucks in Greenwood, the Colored boys, who benefitted from our military training, who were the ones to take up arms against the whites over the objections of the good ones. There's more than one or two like that in *Black Panther*...all hot in the head to go to war against the white race. You should see the weapons they have...and the plans. From the very opening, it's all about revenge, revenge, revenge against the white race. I believe if we let this continue, if we let this motion picture keep playing to a wider and wider audience, especially a Negro audience, we're playing with fire."

It was J. Edgar Hoover who broke the uncomfortable silence that followed Nixon's recitation. "You mentioned the town of Enfield..."

"Enfield...Thompsonville," replied Nixon. "They're the same place. Like New York and Manhattan."

"Well, I know Enfield," said Hoover. "Know of it. That was the home of that troublemaker Paul Robeson. He moved out after Truman lifted his passport for his communist activities. That could be our link...why this is the only goddamn town in the country we're hearing about this movie."

"You think he could've financed a motion picture on a singer's income?" asked Dulles.

"Before we killed his international career," said Hoover, "He was pulling in six figures a year. Now he makes maybe $3,000 annually if he's lucky. But who knows how much he salted away. Or how much his handlers in Moscow may have contributed to this film."

"We should look into this," said Dulles.

"I agree," said Ike, "But let's be quiet about it. Too many mysteries about this damn film for us to be getting too far ahead of ourselves. Dick, I want you to go back to Connecticut and bring that copy of the movie back here so we can get it thoroughly examined."

"But that's one of the strange things about it," argued Nixon. "You can't get into the projection booth to stop it."

"Who can't?" Hoover challenged.

"I don't know," replied Nixon. "The local police. Fire department. They told me they've tried to break the door down and can't."

"Goddammit," said Hoover, "My boys were breaking down the mob's speakeasy doors just for daily exercise. We'll go down and get that damn movie."

"Will you need a warrant?" asked Dulles.

"Not with an FBI badge we won't," Hoover declared, rising from his seat to leave even before Ike dismissed the meeting.

Dulles rose to join him. "I'll have my team check on this Wakanda kingdom. Maybe it's real. Countries sprout up like mushrooms over there."

As Hoover and Dulles walked out together, Ike pulled Nixon over for a quiet moment. "Nice work there, Dick. This could be the card we play against Kefauver in a re-election bid if he's the opposition we draw. Movies trump comic books, I should think."

Nixon smiled, genuinely pleased with himself for anticipating the old general's strategic mind.

"One more thing, Dick," said Ike, "Let's not have any public references to that horrible Tulsa race mess. Christ, we dropped incendiary devices on our own citizens there. Not a good look for the country. The less said about it the better."

Chapter Nine

Town Without Pity?

With the Strand closed down, at least temporarily, the D'Aleo family found itself with more time and less money on its hands. To shore up the family income, Ellie started looking for more shifts rather than fewer at the hospital. To assure that the closure was temporary rather than permanent Leo spent endless hours in conversation with lawyers, government officials, and theater industry contacts. To relieve her boredom, Rosemary was in a constant search for Shep, who seemed to have totally disappeared from her life shortly after the police cordoned off the theater. She had no car for getting around and there was no phone at his mother's house where he lived. She never realized how much the Strand was central to their relationship. They could always count on seeing each other there, spending time together and making plans to go elsewhere, but all of a sudden their relationship had gone as dark as the Strand.

Frustrated and longing to see him she ventured out on foot just on the off chance she would find him. She walked up Grant Street from the family home and then took a right on Rt. 5 on the familiar path she took to high school for four years. When she got to the high school, she just kept walking toward the classic end of town...no shops...no offices...surely no theaters, but a leafy stretch of homes with Georgian columns, colonial-era churches, and historic landmarks of Enfield's pre-Revolutionary period. She ambled, intent at first on possibly catching sight of Shep driving down the town's main thoroughfare. But then she came to a boulder on the side of the road and her mind went elsewhere. The boulder was engraved with the following:

THIS BOULDER MARKS THE PLACE WHERE STOOD THE SECOND MEETING HOUSE OF THE FIRST CHURCH OF CHRIST IN ENFIELD BUILT A.D. 1704 AND USED FOR WORSHIP UNTIL 1775.

IN THIS MEETING HOUSE ON JULY 8, 1741, DURING THE REVIVAL KNOWN AS "THE GREAT AWAKENING" JOHNATHAN EDWARDS PREACHED HIS CELEBRATED SERMON "SINNERS IN THE HANDS OF AN ANGRY GOD"

Of course Rosemary knew "Sinners in the Hands of an Angry God" as did every schoolchild in Enfield. They knew or at least heard of it since it was mandatory reading in the town's junior high. Rosemary had not committed the sermon to memory, but the gist of it was most impressionable on young minds and thus unforgettable: "The bow of God's wrath is bent, and the arrow made ready on the string, and justice bends the arrow at your heart, and strains the bow, and it is nothing but the mere pleasure of God, and that of an angry God, without any promise or obligation at all, that keeps the arrow one moment from being made drunk with your blood."

What was new to Rosemary was the discovery of this boulder marking the spot where Edwards delivered the sermon. She'd never seen it before...never knew it was there. Until that moment, the sermon was as detached from any time and place as any textbook assignment ever was. The idea that a building stood on that spot where former citizens of her hometown gathered and worshipped words that would resound for more than 200 years was revelatory to her. It made her ponder whether such a circumstance existed in her current Enfield. Was there a building in town where words were spoken that would have resonance long after she and all her contemporaries had passed? That profound question shook her being. She had always been so busy at the theater and pleasing her parents and canoodling with Shep that her mind was generally off limits to such deep thoughts. But there she was entertaining such a thought as she turned and started to backtrack her walk.

She hadn't gotten far when she noticed on the opposite side of the street up ahead a broken down, blue painted school bus. She recognized it immediately as one of the buses from the local L.B. Haas tobacco farm where Shep worked before he came to the Strand. She also recognized the torso that disappeared under the hood and bent over the bus's engine as Shep's. She screamed with delight at the sight and ran towards him.

Shep pulled his head out to turn and look in her direction. She ran into his arms, nearly in tears, "Shep...Shep...Shep...where have you been? I've missed you like crazy."

They kissed.

"I'm sorry, hon," he began, "I've been busy with..."

"You're working tobacco!" she exclaimed, suddenly noticing the row of black faces looking down on them from inside the bus.

"Well," he started to explain, "I made a deal with Mr. Granger, my old supervisor there, that I'd take the bus around and pick up Colored folks and bring them by for a tour of the fields. Every summer it gets harder and harder for them to get kids to take on that work; it's so hard and dirty. I told him I would pick these people up from, you know, Springfield and New Haven and so forth and bring them by and then he could pay me a bit per head for however many sign their kids up for the next summer."

"What an extremely weird idea, Shep. What's gotten into you?"

"To be honest, Rosemary, it's a lie," he replied a bit abashed. "I told him that just to get the use of the bus. But it's all really for you. Your dad. The theater."

"What on earth are you talking about?"

He looked up at the people on the bus and waved his hand over them. They all smiled and waved back.

"They want to see *Black Panther*," he said. "So I'm taking them."

"But the police still have the theater roped off, and dad heard this morning that men are coming up from Washington to maybe close the theater for good."

"That's why we're bringing the Underground Railroad back," Shep said. "You see that house," he added, pointing to a large mansion up the road from the bus breakdown. "That's the Potter mansion. Wealthy Ephraim Pease built it next door to his own mansion when his 14-year old daughter Sybil married Rev. Potter in 1779. Even though his father-in-law was a slave owner, that didn't stop Rev. Potter from turning his house into a station on the Underground Railroad to help runaway slaves escape to freedom."

Rosemary looked into Shep's face with unfiltered astonishment. "Shep Farrell," she said, "What's gotten into you? I mean, what in the deepest recesses of all unholy hell has gotten into you?"

Before Shep could answer, Marcus rolled out from under the bus, holding up a small black rubber hose. "Found it!" he announced.

"That's it!" Shep exclaimed. He took the piece from Marcus's hand and rushed over to put it under the hood of the bus.

"I'm Marcus," Marcus said, holding a hand out to Rosemary. She took it tentatively...and not because it would be the first Colored hand she ever touched, but because she was still flabbergasted by the tall Negro's sudden appearance from under the bus.

"Rosemary," she replied. Then she quickly moved toward Shep, who had ducked under the hood again momentarily.

When Shep re-emerged triumphant, he announced, "There, that should do it. Rosemary, Marcus is my new friend. He's helping me get all these people in to see the movie. Come on. We'll give you a ride." With that he hurried in to take the bus driver's seat. Marcus politely ushered her in front of him. As she hesitantly climbed the stairs into the bus, she was greeted by the sound of the engine turning over and an appreciative applause from the bus riders. When Rosemary reached the top step, she was shocked to see another white face against the sea of blacks. It was Mrs. Dundee, her bookkeeping teacher, seated in the front row and acknowledging her with a smile. Marcus slid by and took the seat next to Sheila, as a young Negro boy vacated the seat across the aisle and offered it to Rosemary. Somewhat in a daze she took it.

Shep started motoring north up RT 5 back toward the high school and Rosemary's home, but he hardly travelled a mile when he stopped, pulled over and opened the door. He looked in the rearview mirror back at his passengers and directed their eyes out the door to another stately, old Enfield home. It was grand enough for royalty, fronted by four large white columns; a fancy wrought iron fence balcony overlooking the main entrance, and north and south facing porticoes. Shep said, "Marcus, tell the people about that house."

Marcus gladly stood up and turned back to face the passengers. "That, ladies and gentlemen, was the home of world renown singer Paul Robeson, who lived there from 1941 to just last year. Most of you know the lofty heights Brother Robeson has reached in a world full of challenges for the Colored man…first in his class at Rutgers University, All-American football player, international musical star of the stage, and invited to give a royal command performance at Buckingham Palace."

"Ooohs and aaahs," rippled through the bus.

"And of course," Marcus continued, "Many of you know of his tireless efforts on behalf of the poor and downtrodden. I was honored to be one of his bodyguards in Peekskill, New York, just a few short years ago when he was forced to reschedule a benefit concert for union workers after the Ku Klux Klan broke up the original concert. We linked arms…black and white together…to protect him while he sang his heart out for 25,000 working people from all over. I will not tell you it was an easy day in the sun, because it was not. The enemies of the common good attacked again…viciously…while the police stood idly by. No, it was not an easy day, but it was a proud day, and I'd do it again to bring about a better day. When you're watching this glorious movie tonight just a few miles from here, I want you to remember this house and the brave man who lived here because that movie owes him a debt."

Marcus responded to the respectful silence that followed by walking down the aisle of the bus and pressing the flesh of the passengers.

Rosemary leaned forward in her seat to ask Shep, "Where exactly are we going?"

Shep smiled and said, "Well, first to Haas Tobacco. Got to keep up appearances, and got to stay out of sight as much as possible 'til dark. If you know what I mean."

Rosemary looked at Marcus heading back down the aisle, exchanged a cursory smile with Sheila, and then turned to Shep. "I really don't know how you can afford to do this. How can you even afford the gas?"

"Everyone chips in," he replied. "They bring their own lunches. So it doesn't cost a dime. Which reminds me." He reached down to the side of his seat, picked up a bulging moneybag and handed it to Rosemary. "Proceeds from ticket sales. These are paying customers, sweetheart."

"Your man's the White Panther, Rosemary," said Marcus as he resumed his seat. Shep smiled proudly and touched down on the gas pedal, sending the bus forward. So intent were they in going unnoticed that they didn't notice less than another mile up the road the two black, government-issued limousines disgorging

passengers...six white men in topcoats, suits and hats...checking into

the esteemed Elmcroft Inn, formerly Vail's Sanatorium for the

treatment of mental illnesses.

Chapter Ten

A Shot in the Dark...

And then Another and Another...

Within minutes of taking their respective leaves of the Oval Office, both FBI Director J. Edgar Hoover and Vice President Richard M. Nixon determined that it would behoove them to be part of the Washington contingency to Thompsonville to confiscate the rogue film *Black Panther*. For Hoover the mission provided an opportunity for a remake of his last bittersweet experience with crime fighting at a movie theater. In 1934 it was his FBI that tracked gangster John Dillinger to the Biograph Theater in Chicago and shot him dead outside it. But it was his agent Marvin Purvis who got all the credit. "One day they're going to make a goddamn action movie about that stunted punk," Hoover would complain to close associates, "And I'm going to go down as an underwear-sniffing desk jockey." If this time headlines were going to be made at a movie theater, he was going to be there...so he vowed to Clyde Tolson, his intimate associate, roommate, and chief beneficiary of his will, though not his homosexual lover as his admirers insisted. To assure there were headlines, he contacted his favorite media functionary, Walter Winchell, who led his next radio broadcast with his usual breathless sensationalism this way: "Good evening, Mr. and Mrs. America, from border to border and coast to coast and all the ships at sea. Let's go to press. This reporter has it on reliable word that the nation's top G-Man and crime fighter J. Edgar Hoover himself is traveling to Anytown USA this week...A.K.A. Thompsonville, Connecticut...to confiscate a film that confidential sources suggest may be used by communist infiltrators to foment racial unrest here in the land of the free and the home of the brave. More to come as details unfold."

Nixon was just as intent on being on the scene, and had sworn to himself that no picture would be taken in Thompsonville that didn't feature him holding the confiscated film. It would be the "Pumpkin Papers" all over again, where he had been photographed holding microfilm hidden in a hollowed-out pumpkin that was later used to convict alleged communist spy Alger Hiss of perjury. That photo had helped launch his national political profile as a commie fighter, and he imagined getting a similar boost if he could claim to be the man who saved America from coast-to-coast race riots. As he packed his bag for Thompsonville, he thought of the publicity of Kefauver's comic book hearings and cackled at the idea of such a big shot frying such small fish. He thought of Ike's mortality and shuddered at the morbid possibilities. He thought of his insatiable, fevered ambitions and felt the unmistakable pull of an erection.

Nixon and Hoover checked into the Elmcroft Inn with four of Hoover's agents, Flint, Stone, Steele, and Cole. As the director had promised, the four were all veterans of the Bureau's gang-busting Prohibition days, with plenty of experience swinging axes and sledgehammers at doors built for resistance. When told they might have to take down a projection booth in a small town movie theater, they all reacted like veteran major league ball players invited to play in a Sunday beer league. They were giddy with excitement.

Giddy might also best describe the audience across town at the Strand that had gathered for the after-midnight showing of *Black Panther*. It had been a particularly good day of preliminaries with some of the participants being so taken with old Granger's pitch about work in the tobacco fields that they actually committed their kids to work there the following summer. "You may make some money out of this after all," Rosemary told Shep with a loving nudge.

But with the audience comfortably in their seats and the film just beginning to roll, things suddenly began to go bad...very bad. Milo, who had been reliably absent from inside the theater for the duration of Shep's underground railroad exploits, got word that the Feds were in town to confiscate the film and he realized this night could be his last chance to see it. Niggers or not, he had to see for himself if it was as spectacular and thrilling a movie as everyone was saying it was. When he entered the theater, the film's dark opening scenes did not provide him with enough illumination to identify the two people he encountered standing at the back of the theater. All he knew was that no one should even have been there regardless of who they were, and it was his job to toss them out. He immediately grabbed for his flashlight and turned it on. The flash of his light over the faces of the two transgressors sent him into shock. That was quickly followed by rage. "You Nigger lover!" he screamed at Sheila. "You motherfucker!" he screamed at Marcus.

"Milo! Please..." his mother yelled back.

But too late...too little. Milo drew his service revolver on duty for the first time in his fledgling police career and started firing. The *Black Panther* audience went into full panic with people jumping out of their seats, hiding under their seats, running as fast as they could to get away from their seats. It was utter mayhem until Shep managed to circle around behind Milo and hammer him across the back of the head with a fire extinguisher.

When Rosemary turned the house lights up, the toll of the evening became apparent. Milo was unconscious. Two audience members were seriously wounded. And Sheila and Marcus both appeared to have been shot dead. Shep was down on his knees in anguish and sorrow, knowing that much of the disaster laid out before his horrified eyes was solely due to his good intentions.

Chapter Eleven

After Hours

The shots fired from Milo's gun and the screaming of the scattering, frightened Negroes alerted the desk sergeant at the Enfield Police Department a few doors down from the Strand. The call went out and soon the theater was filled with police, firemen, town officials, and the local news reporter. It's not that everyone was on high alert for such an incident, but that everyone involved lived pretty close to the center of town, and it took not one of them more than 10 minutes to answer the phone, put on their pants, and drive over to the theater.

Still, all that readiness prepared none of them for fully comprehending what had happened. Milo returned to consciousness and claimed he had come upon intruders and opened fire. Shep apologized for hitting Milo with the fire extinguisher, explaining that he was trying to save lives from flying bullets. Rosemary said that the Negroes were there simply to watch the movie. The police chief said he wasn't taking any chances and ordered a round up of the fleeing Negroes and their detention in the youth center from the police station.

A few hours later Hoover and his FBI agents were on the case and after back and forth with bureau headquarters in DC were able to identify Marcus as one of the bodyguards for Paul Robeson at Peekskill, which made its way out of Hoover's mouth as "agitator Paul Robeson" and "Peekskill race riot." Which is how the local reporter heard it and reported it and how it was picked up by the national media, including Walter Winchell: "Good evening, Mr. and Mrs. America, from border to border and coast to coast and all the ships at sea. Let's go to press. As this reporter told you two days ago top G-Man J. Edgar Hoover was off to Smalltown USA…A.K.A. Thompsonville, Connecticut…on the hunt for a film that threatened to provoke nationwide racial unrest. Once again, J. Edgar arrived just in the nick of time and was able to put down a race riot, but not before a Negro agitator with communist ties and his hostage, a local white woman, were shot and killed."

Sheila had gone from a woman who had cuckolded her husband to a woman who was raped and kidnapped by a Colored communist after her husband Ralph arrived on the scene and told that version to anyone who would listen...which was a lot of people.

While the national media was beating the drums for one version of events, the drumbeats coming out of Negro communities up and down the East Coast told another. In their telling, a fabulous motion picture of Negro pride and liberation was being suppressed by the authorities, and the Colored man who had heroically tried to unchain that film had been shot and killed by police.

Beat...

Beat...

Beat...

The tribal drums were setting in motion plans for street demonstrations in protest.

Nixon was not happy with how any of this was unfolding. He wanted to position himself as the one who prevented murder, mayhem, and rioting, but with all of that seemingly underway right under his nose he was left on the sidelines, as Hoover became the action figure.

Hoover's action led him to take his detail of agents to the Strand. He was right about not needing a warrant. He didn't even need to show his FBI badge. Leo was so eager to be done with *Black Panther* that he would've been happy to have the bank foreclose on him. He thought seriously about taking the money Shep had made with his underground showings of the film and moving the entire family to Florida for a fresh start in land speculation.

Hoover took his men up to the projection booth where he unleashed them on the door. Stone and Steele attacked it first with the sledgehammers. They pounded away for a half hour, first to good-natured joshing from Flint and Cole but then to angry goading from Hoover. "Goddamn it! Goddamn it! Is it time for you buttercups to take your pensions? Flint! Cole! Get your axes over here!"

Bored with Stone and Steele's futility, Flint and Cole had turned around to watch *Black Panther*, which of course was still running. "That looks like a hell of a picture," Cole commented, drawing a quick, derisive sneer from Hoover. Then Flint and Cole replaced Stone and Steele and proceeded to repeat their futility for another 30 minutes. That's when Hoover sent Stone and Steele out for drills. "Lots of them," he said. "Every damn drill in this goddamn town."

The agents returned with a plethora of drills...a pistol grip electric drill, a pneumatic drill, a hammer drill, even an old hand-operated "eggbeater" drill that they agreed to not show Hoover except as a last resort. And then they brought in a jackhammer and took turns trying to hammer their way through the floor and under the door. But the projection booth was impervious, and the *Black Panther* movie rolled on. Finally, Flint turned to Hoover and said, "What do you think about a few explosive charges, Chief?"

Hoover, completely out of patience, didn't hesitate, "Go get 'em."

They did, and then:

Boom 1!

Boom 2!

Boom 3!

The door didn't budge; the projection booth remained intact.

Hoover would never have admitted defeat, but Nixon had been hanging around and watching in amazement at what was happening. He was amazed not only at the seemingly indestructible projection booth, but that the fickle finger of fate seemed to have pointed his way again. Hoover's evident frustration meant that the problem of the rogue movie was now one that required more connivance than action. Without saying a word to Hoover, he sent a telegram to Eisenhower detailing the difficulties Hoover was encountering and suggesting that the next best route to take was to set up an executive command post there in the Strand with Nixon in charge of a thoroughgoing frame-by-frame analysis of the movie.

Ike telegraphed back, "Dick, you're the one *STOP*"

Chapter Twelve

The Unusual Suspects

When Nixon got the go-ahead from Ike to put together an executive committee to examine *Black Panther*, he had immediately put in a call to Pat asking her to bring him up his flannel pajamas in anticipation of cooler New England nights. The driver dropped Pat off directly at the Strand where Nixon was overseeing its conversion into an executive hearing room. Carpenters had built ersatz conference tables over the backs of theater seats, klieg lights had been rolled in, witness chairs had been lined up down in front of the screen. All this while *Black Panther* continued to play on the screen and dominate the room both visually and audibly. The challenges were severely testing Nixon who fancied himself a match for any crisis.

Pat approached him with his PJs and received her customary peck on the cheek. She looked up at the screen where she watched a bald-headed African woman fight off multiples of armed angry men. Nixon looked at his wife and saw an unusual glimmer in her eye that made him instantly uncomfortable. He grabbed his pajamas from her and said, "Thank you, Pat. You can go now. Kiss the girls for me."

She looked at him and then took a glance around at the manufactured chaos of the movie theater. "Why don't you just make a movie of the movie and take it back to Washington with you?"

The question hit him like a kick in the nuts and he showed it. He walked her out to the waiting car, then went back into the theater and called a halt to everything. "Someone get me a camera and a good cameraman," he ordered to no one in particular.

A week later, Nixon's executive committee investigation into the film *Black Panther* was meeting under proper conditions in the basement of the White House. The Committee consisted of Hoover; the Dulles brothers; Prescott Bush; and Walt Disney. Walt was not only a friend and supporter of the administration and an expert on filmmaking but he had once helped the Motion Picture Alliance for the Preservation of American Ideals produce a pamphlet warning how moviemakers should avoid subversive influences in their films, to wit:

- Don't smear the free-enterprise system
- Don't smear industrialists

- Don't smear wealth
- Don't smear the profit motive
- Don't deify the "common man"
- Don't glorify "the collective"

Ike served as an *ex-officio* member and promised to be available as needed. The committee's secondhand copy of the film was mounted on a projector at the back of the room and the committee table faced a movie screen at the front. A stenographer and projectionist were present. As much as Nixon wanted a reporter and photographer there from the national press, he knew he couldn't really have them without giving additional exposure to a film he was trying to suppress.

The first time someone called for the film to be stopped for discussion was when the African kingdom of Wakanda was mentioned and Disney raised a hand and asked, "Is Wakanda a real place?"

"No," John Foster Dulles immediately replied.

"Though it could be code for a real place," his brother added.

Seconds later, Disney asked for another stop when the film narration mentioned the precious metal unique to Wakanda known as vibranium. "Is vibranium real?" he asked.

"No," said John Foster Dulles.

"Not that we know of," added Allen Dulles.

"Gentlemen," said Nixon, "This is a damn long movie. At this rate we're only going to make it longer. Hard to tell at this stage what's real and what's not about it, so how about if we keep our ongoing discussions to the big questions: Is it a national security threat? Where does it come from? Who's behind it? Why can't we stop it from playing at that theater or penetrate that projection booth? Jot down any other questions you may have and we'll address them at the end." He looked around the room for compliance and then looked at the projectionist and nodded.

As soon as the scene titled onscreen as *Oakland 1992* started to unfold, Hoover stopped the film. "There's the answer to your national security question. You see those guns, and did you hear who those Negroes are plotting against? 'The Feds'. That's us."

"Good point," said Prescott Bush.

"Make a note of that," Nixon told the stenographer. "Roll it," he told the projectionist.

But no sooner did the film start rolling again then came another order to stop it as the Marvel Studios logo appeared.

"Well, now we know where it came from," said Nixon. "Walt, any ideas about this Marvel Studios?"

The world's foremost cartoonist pondered the question and then said, "Marvel has something to do with comic books. They're not in the movie business. Just an organizational umbrella, as far as I know, for a lot of cheap crime and horror stuff."

"Like the ones Kefauver is investigating?" asked Bush.

"Exactly," said Nixon. "Maybe this is payback."

"Payback," exclaimed Bush. "He just held those hearings a few months ago. It's not possible to put out something like this as payback."

Hoover chimed in, "Why call it payback? This seems like more of an attempt to subvert our youth, even if it's just the Colored youth. This could be part of a grand strategy that goes hand in hand with the comic books. I'll get my guys to look in on this Marvel business. We'll see what Kefauver has on it too."

"Good," said Nixon. "Let's get back to it."

The movie rolled on again with comments made in passing.

When the character Okoye told the African women she and the Black Panther had just rescued, "You will speak nothing of this day" Nixon told the stenographer, "Make a note of that."

When the character Shuri gave her brother the Black Panther "the finger" Prescott Bush said, "The insouciance of that gesture just frosts me."

"Insouciance, sir?" asked the stenographer.

"Yes. Put it down," Bush told her.

And when the character Killmonger first appeared with his Africanized hair tied into a sprout at the top, John Foster Dulles asked, "What are we to make of that Alfalfa hair-do?"

"He needs Ike's barber," his brother answered, and the room burst out into laughter.

But the laughter was cut short when Secretary of State Dulles raised his hand to stop the film. Killmonger was just accusing the white female museum curator of stealing artifacts. "Listen to this. Rewind and play that part again," he told the projectionist. After they did, he repeated the offending line for the benefit of the room, "'How do you think your ancestors got all these? Do you think they paid a fair price or did they take it like they took everything else?' That right there is the essence of the anti-colonial message that is shaking the globe, gentlemen. I think we're getting a clearer idea of the agenda."

"Well taken, brother," said the CIA Director Dulles. "We've got more than juvenile delinquency to worry about here."

They let the film roll through the large Wakanda gathering on the cliffs overlooking the spectacular array of waterfalls for the battle of succession between T'Challa, the Black Panther, and J'bari, his rival. Like everyone else who had seen the scene for the first time even this group of sober government investigators was mesmerized by the colors, the sounds, and the thrill of the wrestling match, which transcended any fight any of them had ever seen anywhere. When the scene ended with T'Challa's victory, Nixon ordered a stop of the film and turned to Disney. "Walt, you're the movie expert here. How did they do that fight on top of the waterfall? Is that trick photography?"

Disney shook his head and said, "Well, it's got to be *some* kind of trick, Dick. The whole scene is a trick. There's no way they put all those people up on the walls of those cliffs, and it sure wasn't done on some studio backlot. And you don't put a camera crew and actors on such a dangerous waterfall and get anything out of it that looks as good as that. I'd have to give this to some of my technical people to study."

"We'll make you a copy," said Nixon.

The film began again, but not for long. As soon as South Korea was mentioned and the location switched to Busan, the group made a communal gasp. They were speechless as the film's glittery, pulsating image of Korea played out, moving in full throttle action from swank gambling club to skyscraper studded streets.

"Korea!" John Foster Dulles finally exclaimed. "Korea is a hellhole, barely digging itself out of war. What's the point of this? And what's Busan?"

"Must mean Pusan," his brother answered. "Maybe a typo."

"With all this technology, you think they made a typo?" asked Bush.

"Prescott," asked Hoover, always the grand inquisitor, "I thought you saw this movie before. You didn't notice the whole Korea thing?"

"I got so wrapped up in the car chase, I forgot."

"I don't know what the hell to make of this," said Nixon. "Is this somebody's idea of Korea in the future?"

"If it is," said John Foster Dulles, "Somebody's got a pretty wild imagination."

"And a lot of that reefer madness went into this," said his brother to haughty huffs all around.

"You can say that again," said Hoover. "You saw that scene with him taking the 'heart-shaped herb', didn't you? Strong evidence of heavy reefer madness behind this movie, I can tell you that."

The group was mightily perplexed by the Korea business and rather emotionally exhausted by the over-stimulating car chase through the Korean streets, so they agreed to take a lunch break. Over tuna sandwiches and Cokes they took off their investigator hats and put on their just plain moviegoer caps and commented mostly about the cinematic elements of the film.

"The acting's not half bad," said Bush. "The men remind me a lot of Harry Belafonte."

"Yes," said Allen Dulles, "but I'd like to see more Lena Horne than all those baldy girls."

"I don't know if you could ever see more of Lena Horne than you see of all those baldies," said his brother, and they all snorted at his meaning.

"That music," said Nixon.

"Pure African jungle," said Hoover. "It's that wild stuff they love. Gets them all hot and moving around and aggressive. I don't like it. Not one bit."

"Walt, you've been pretty quiet through all this," said Nixon.

"Yes, well, I'm just trying to figure out how they did most of it. The music and colors and stunts, the animation, it's all so beyond anything we've ever seen, even in this second generation version. Wish I could see the real thing."

"We can send you to downtown Thompsonville, Connecticut, whenever you want," Nixon told him. "But don't expect a fantasyland. They welcomed me with a damned carpet swatch. It's a very dull place, which raises the question again, *this* movie...*there*? Why?"

"And I'll tell you again," said Hoover, "It's Robeson. He's behind it."

"Maybe so," said Nixon. "Let's get back to it and see if we can find any more clues."

They watched in silence until the Black Panther took wounded Agent Ross of the CIA to Wakanda for the bullet in his spine. Then a line of dialog pricked their ears and Bush repeated it. "*Another white boy to fix*. Hear that?" he said. "Very disrespectful...and contemptuous."

"Contemptuous?" asked the stenographer.

"Put it down," said Bush.

When Ross came out of his surgery and asked, "How long ago was Korea?" Allen Dulles said, "I think they're playing with us now."

It wasn't until Shuri, the female character who saved Ross's life, called him a "colonizer" and Ross identified ostensible villain

Killmonger as an American agent who specialized in destabilizing foreign governments that they stopped the film again. "Fuck!" exclaimed CIA Director Dulles. "*Destabilizing foreign governments. It's as if this goddamn movie has gotten hold of our confidential files.*"

Nixon stepped in front of the movie screen to address the committee. "I think it's all becoming clear now, gentlemen, isn't it? In the gambling club scene, the Americans are introduced as an enemy. Then the disparaging 'white boy' remark. We learn that the character who was plotting violent action against the Feds in the beginning was radicalized by what he saw in America...and then this, this outright betrayal of our foreign policy. There can be no doubt that the intent of this film is to spread anti-colonial agitation to the United States...to provoke our native Negroes to see themselves as oppressed by the white race and to take up arms against it. I think we can all agree that we're dealing with a very serious national security threat here."

The soberness of Nixon's pronouncement permeated the room and created a profound silence. But then Disney shuffled slightly in his seat, cleared his throat, and spoke, "There is a lot of talk about peace though. The Wakandans do say they don't like war."

"*Some* Wakandans," said John Foster Dulles. "The film is setting up an obvious Marxist dialectic between those who want to strike out at the world violently and those who want to subtly subvert it. But make no mistake, *Wakanda Forever* is the ultimate goal."

They ran the rest of the film to the end, and took the final, wry smile of the Black Panther in close-up before an international assembly as a confirmation of their findings.

"See that smirk?" asked Hoover. "It's all a typical communist ruse."

As the credits started to roll, Nixon ordered the stenographer to get down all the names that appeared for further investigation. Then he began explaining where they would go from there...that they would gather up everyone's notes and collate them to prepare an executive summary for Ike. He talked about timelines and future subcommittee meetings and plenary sessions. He was totally oblivious to the thousands of names scrolling by on the credits behind him and the stenographer who was madly trying to jot them all down. Until finally the cameraman who had kept the film rolling through the credits with the sound turned down yelled out, "Holy shit!"

They all turned from Nixon to the cameraman, who immediately rewound the film slightly and then motioned for the group to look back at the screen. He hit play forward again, but he might just as well have hit each of them over the head with a hammer for the shock of what they saw next. In the seemingly endless scroll of credits, the following line appeared in bold white lettering:

Walt Disney Studios

All eyes sharply turned on Disney, who could do nothing but utter, "What the hell?"

Chapter Thirteen

Apocalypse Now?

Ike sat at his desk pondering the document he'd been given entitled Executive Summary of Ad Hoc Committee on The National Security Threat Posed by the Theatrical Film Black Panther. He looked over his glasses at Richard M. Nixon and J. Edgar Hoover, authors of the summary, sitting across from him, and with barely concealed displeasure said, "So you've arrested Walt Disney?"

"Not arrested really," Nixon was quick to clarify.

"We have him under surveillance," added Hoover.

"How did Walt respond to this connection between him and this movie?" Ike asked.

"Said he didn't know anything about it. Said he'd have to ask his brother Roy about it," said Nixon. "But I have tell you, Mr. President, he seemed mighty uncomfortable watching that movie with us. As if he'd rather be somewhere else."

"You mean like in California overseeing his new multi-million dollar project, Disneyland?" Ike asked, with more than a touch of sarcasm.

"I get what you're saying, Mr. President," said Nixon, "But that's just it. No one else in the country has the technology, creative resources, and money to pull off a movie like this Black Panther thing."

"Certainly not that agitating Negro Robeson," said Hoover. "Even if he was valedictorian at Rutgers."

"Rutgers," Nixon scoffed. "We think this could all be a promotion for Disneyland. This may be the movie version of that Tomorrowland of his."

"Mixed with radical politics," Hoover added.

"So a big, expensive promotion for a theme park built around Negro rights and aspirations. You ever know Walt to do anything for Negroes?" the President asked.

After a brief pause, Nixon ventured, "That Uncle Remus movie."

"The *Zip a Dee Doo Dah* one," Hoover added helpfully.

Ike carefully placed their executive summary down on his desk and removed his reading glasses. "Let me tell you something, gentlemen. While you were preoccupied watching the movie and writing your report, I was busy looking for the answer to the bigger question: Why was that theater's projection booth so impenetrable to every effort to break into it? So I called in a favor from Albert Einstein." And at that Ike cast a sharp warning look at Hoover, who had tried to keep Einstein from immigrating to America. Hoover bit his tongue, and Ike continued. "I asked this valuable resource of *ours* to go up there to Connecticut...undercover of course...and see what he could learn about that projection booth. And you know what he told me? He told me it's actually coated with a material that is not from this planet. It's from outer space."

Nixon and Hoover quickly exchanged looks of *ah-ha*, and said in unison, "Vibranium!"

"Yes," said Ike, "It would seem that this metal you write about in your summary that's bulletproof and can be shaped into a spear point that could stop a tank and that you dismiss as not real is in fact real."

"But what about Disney? His name was on it," said Nixon.

"Obviously a frame-up," said Hoover. "It's easily done. I've done it a thousand times."

"So we let him go?" asked Nixon.

"Let Walt go make his money," said Ike. "He's on our side."

"And Robeson?" asked Hoover.

"He can't make money, can he?" said Ike. "If he can't make money he can't hurt anybody. Certainly not the United States of America."

"So this changes everything," said Nixon.

"It does. It means we're not just dealing with an elaborate propaganda threat…or theme park promotion film," said the President, "but with a material threat to our national security."

"Jesus. It's as if Cuba went communist", said Nixon, "and allowed the Russians to point missiles at us from 90 miles away. But this would be worse…right here on the American continent in an American town…under control of forces we can't see and with a purpose we can't assess. But why this town? Why Thompsonville, Connecticut?"

"Face it," answered Ike, "if it'd been any other town in America, except maybe New York, we'd be asking the same question. "Why Dubuque? Duquesne? Ashtabula?"

"Did Einstein have any ideas on how to deal with this, sir?" asked Hoover.

"He's working on a theory he says, but we don't have time for that," said Ike. "I'm ordering the total demolition of the Strand theater in Thompsonville, Connecticut. Maybe we've been attacking that projection booth from the wrong angle. Maybe we should be coming at it from the outside in…expose and isolate it."

Hoover jumped in to say, "At the very least we eliminate the screen and seats so it'll be impossible to view the movie again. Very tactical, Mr. President."

"Yes," said Ike, "And once we've eliminated the brick and mortar surrounding it, we can pinpoint it and strike with the best weapon at our command."

"The H-bomb!" exalted Nixon. "Yes!"

Chapter Fourteen

This Boy's Life

Shep had disappeared around about the time word spread through Thompsonville that for national security purposes President Eisenhower had ordered the demolition of the Strand. The circle of people who were concerned about Shep's disappearance was relatively small, however, consisting mostly of Shep's mother and Rosemary. His mom believed he'd gone looking for a new job out of state and Shep being Shep had simply forgotten to tell her. Rosemary, who was more attuned to the emotions the interdiction of *Black Panther* had aroused, feared more serious circumstances. She was worried that those who saw Shep as a white knight...or, rather, a White Panther...had somehow seduced him into helping them further fight against the prohibition. But because emotions had risen just as high on the other side of the issue, she also worried that there were those who saw Shep as an instigator of Negro unrest and had done something nefarious to him.

Like everything else the authorities faced in regards to *Black Panther*, the demo of the Strand had not gone smoothly. The first day, they attempted to bring it down the customary way with a wrecking ball attached to a crane. As a huge crowd gathered...most of the town actually...the crane operator swung the wrecking ball at the left front of the unimposing building for much of an hour without making a dent. The crane operator then spent much of the rest of the day maneuvering around and about the building in hopes of finding a sweet spot. By day's end, the Strand remained standing with nary a dent.

The next day the government sent in an explosives crew who lined as much of the Strand that was exposed with dynamite. Warnings and apologies were issued to surrounding buildings and businesses, which was good because after the plunger was pushed and the dynamite exploded the only buildings affected were the neighboring ones. The Strand stood strong and stout, good as it ever was.

On day 3, Ike dispatched a couple of the Sherman tanks he had come to rely so much upon while leading the allies in World War II. The crowd had swollen to urban enormity for the arrival of the tanks. As it was winter, the Mill Pond was frozen over with ice, so much of the overflow crowd of spectators stood on the ice to watch the tanks do their damage. Vendors on skates snaked in and out of the gathering, selling chocolate Yoo-hoo and roasted chestnuts, feeding the festive atmosphere. But when the tanks fired on the Strand, their shells exploded meekly against the building and then ricocheted, showering over the crowd on the ice and inciting a stampede. As the crowd thundered over the ice, it began to crack and within minutes hundreds of Thompsonvillians were falling into the icy water. The entire demo of the Strand being conducted before newsreel cameras and TV crews turned the sudden, massive rescue operation into an immense embarrassment for the Eisenhower Administration.

Fortunately no one drowned in the ice break because as big as the crowd was on the ice it was even bigger off so there were plenty on hand to help with the rescue. But the political embarrassment led to a determination that the Strand was coming down no matter what it took. Eyewitness reports that bombers at nearby Westover Air Force Base had been put on QAA (Quick Action Alert) fueled rumors that Ike might be planning to drop the H-Bomb on Thompsonville. Recent headlines about H-bomb testing on the Marshall Islands that resulted in radiation exposure and relocation for hundreds of people placed such a scenario well within the ever-broadening realm of apocalyptic possibility. Townspeople began to casually ruminate on where they might end up in the event of a relocation...fantasies about government subsidized bungalows on Florida beaches were not uncommon.

Rosemary was having none of it. She had become increasingly anxious about Shep's whereabouts. So much so that when she picked up the Strand's mail at the post office, she skipped right over any moral qualms she might have had and immediately opened a piece of mail clearly labeled with Shep's name as sender. It had been addressed to Edward R. Morrow (sic), CBS News, New York, New York. Apparently someone along the line of delivery couldn't figure out that Edward R. Morrow was Edward R. Murrow and stamped the letter *Return to Sender*. Rosemary opened it and read the one page letter written in Shep's distinctive scrawl:

Dear Sir:

My name is Shep Farrell. I'm the projectionist at the Strand Theater in Thompsonville, Connecticut. A movie called Black Panther has been playing nonstop here for months. We have just heard that the US goverment has decided that the movie is a thread to the country and plans on recking the Strand to stop anyone else from seeing it. I have seen this movie more times than anyone, hundreds, and I can tell you from my heart that it is not a threat. It is a movie that gives Negro people a positive image of theirselves as heroes and fighters and people of good will and intellegence. My colored friend Marcus was killed trying to help other Negroes get to see this movie. He believed it was the best thing that had happened to colored people in America since the Emancipation Proclamation by President Abraham Lincoln. It is for Marcus and all the other Negroes who would like to see this movie and would love it that I'm doing what I'm telling you I'm going to do hear in this letter. I'm going to chain myself to the inside of the Strand so the goverment can't demolish it. I hope this is news. I know you have your hands full with that Joe McCarthy bum but I think it would be good if you could tell the story of Black Panther too.

Sincerly,

Shep Farrell

Rosemary crumbled the letter and pushed it into her purse and then made a mad, fearful dash for the Strand. When she arrived, she was immediately relieved to see that the guard had been let down around the theater. So alarming were the reports of imminent bombing that no one in or out of authority wanted to go near it. She let herself in and ran into the auditorium where she found *Black Panther* still playing and a seriously debilitated, nearly deranged Shep stuck in his own waste chained to a trio of seats in the very middle of all aisles. "Shep!" she screamed. "Shep…Shep…dear, Shep." She bent down to lift his head and looked into his half-lidded eyes. "The key, Shep. Where's the key?"

"Did I save it? Did I save the Strand?" he asked in a half-whisper.

"Yes," she said. "Now we have to save you. Tell me where the key is."

"Under the seat," he said.

Rosemary put her hand under the seat but could only feel a big wad of gum. She peeled it away, and the key came with it. She unglued it from the gum and unlocked Shep's chains and helped lift him to his feet. He tried to force his eyes fully open, but when they caught sight of the movie screen they opened wide on their own accord. Rosemary followed his widened gaze and her own eyes followed suit. The full color spectrum of *Black Panther* was no longer playing out on screen. In its place was the black and white opening title sequence for *Creature from the Black Lagoon* accompanied by an ominous soundtrack. Rosemary looked back and up at the projection booth. She gently put Shep back down in his seat. "I'll be right back," she promised.

She ran up to the projection booth and tried the door. It opened easily. She stepped inside and looked out at the screen where a scientist and two native boys were discovering a large, fossilized claw. She snapped the off button on the camera and the film stopped. She snapped it on and the film started rolling again. When a giant, fresh, creepy claw reached out of the lagoon, she ran back to Shep.

She helped him out of the seat and up the aisle and out the door of the theater. When they got out to the sidewalk, Shep collapsed. A plane flew overhead, and she let out a scream. Rosemary dropped down to tend to Shep and soon others came running...Cap Kelly; Father O'Boyle; Milo Dundee, fresh from his suspension; the General overseeing the demolition; her mother and father. They all stood around Shep as she pleaded, "*Black Panther* is gone. It's over. You have to stop the bombing. Everything's normal again. Stop the madness! Please."

Cap Kelly ran into the theater and quickly returned. "Rosemary's right. *Creature from the Black Lagoon* is now playing."

"I'll call the President," the General announced and jogged off.

Then they all looked down at Shep. "He needs a doctor," Rosemary cried, "Someone get the doctor!" Bursting with love and concern and newfound respect, she looked down at Shep.

He lifted his head slightly and said softly, "Wakanda forever." Then he closed his eyes and died in Rosemary's arms.

Chapter Fifteen

Curse of the Black Panther

The Strand theater did not immediately go the way of the dinosaur, as Leo D'Aleo feared it would. After the Great Black Panther scare of 1954, it survived long enough to still enjoy a few moments of glory at the heart of Enfield's cultural life. For a raucous, joyful gathering of almost all the town's children it was the scene of a live appearance by the entire cast of *The Howdy Doody Show,* which stayed around just long enough for a roll call of all its familiar catchphrases: "Howdy doody!" "Kowabunga!" "Say, kids, what time is it?"

Once a year, the Strand, in mending its fences with the Catholic Church, offered special showings of *Our Lady of Fátima* and *Song of Bernadette*...and in the casual nullification of the Constitution's separation of church and state that was common in the day, the public schools would offer early release for any child who wished to attend such weekday matinees.

The Strand even got to feature at least one 3-D film before the fad faded—ironically enough it was *Revenge of the Creature*, the sequel to *Creature from the Black Lagoon.*

But none of that...not Howdy Doody, not our Lady of Fátima, not even the Creature in 3-D could save Thompsonville from a seemingly relentless series of catastrophes. While none were as dramatic as would have been Eisenhower dropping an H-bomb on it, each in its own way pushed the town closer to collapse. In 1955, the floodwaters of the Connecticut River rose up and roared down Main Street where thousands had lined up to see *Black Panther* less than a year earlier. By the early 1960s, the Bigelow-Sanford Carpet Company, which had once employed as many as 9,000 of the town's residents, laid off most of them, cut production, and moved to the greener pastures of the non-union South. In the early 1970s what was then gloriously billed as the largest shopping mall in the USA was built just a few short miles away from the Strand, ultimately turning Thompsonville's commercial center into a ghost town where even St. Patrick's Church had to compete with less gothic churches for parishioners.

Despite obvious causes for all those events, the residents of the town couldn't help but revert to the superstitious natures that had followed their families from the old countries and they fell into believing that somehow the town's slow but steady decline was due to the brief, sudden appearance of *Black Panther* at their local theater in 1954. It became known, at least quietly within their homes and strictly among family and friends, as the "Curse of the Black Panther". And evidence of the curse could not only be found in the downward spiral of the town, but in the lives of nearly everyone who had been touched by the wild film…locally and beyond.

The D'Aleos lost a two-year lawsuit against their insurance company, which had refused to cover them for their losses during the disruption, arguing that the *Black Panther* event was an "Act of God" for which the company had no liability. Leo tried to sell the family story to *Look Magazine*, but the US Government classified the entire episode as Top Secret, making it as closely guarded and tantalizing a secret as whatever happens at Area 51, the mysterious military base in the Nevada desert.

The curse wasn't just limited to the little people either. Eisenhower's grandson David married Nixon's daughter Julie, and thus the old General, to his great dismay, was forced to spend every holiday for the rest of his life in Nixon's company.

Nixon's overweening ambition led him to the Watergate scandal, which led him to resign the presidency he had schemed for all his life.

Hoover died, and as he feared was remembered mostly as an underwear-sniffing desk jockey.

The Dulles brothers put an indelible family stamp on America's foreign policy and image through their diplomatic and clandestine intrigues, deceptions, manipulations and disdain for the sovereignty of other countries, ushering in a 75-year era of mutual mistrust, crises, and waste of blood and treasure among the US and its international friends and rivals.

The Bushes, Prescott and George Herbert Walker, would become grandfather and father respectively of George W. Bush, whose astonishing record of failure at all levels of life culminated in his becoming the 43rd and Worst President in American History. Luring thousands of young people from towns like Enfield to their deaths in a misbegotten mission of revenge for the terrorist attacks on 9-11 should have secured for him forever the title as America's King of All Failures. But a mere eight years after leaving office, he blew that enormous distinction as well to an even bigger loser, the 45th president of the United States. The curse was merciless.

It was also relentless. Fr. O'Boyle escaped it for three decades with the help of the Catholic Church hierarchy that stealthily moved him from parish to parish whenever accusations arose against his proclivity for pedophilia. Yet when his name came up in an investigation into Church sexual abuse, it was not as a perpetrator but as a victim. The shame and guilt that haunted O'Boyle throughout his life far exceeded whatever discomfort he felt watching *Black Panther*. But O'Boyle's suffering paled to that of his mentor and first seducer, Archbishop O'Brien, who got word he'd been fingered by the law just as he was trying to blow out the candles for his 90th birthday. O'Brien went on to spend every day of the last year of his life watching youth groups, charitable foundations and civic honors in his name renounced and hearing his name become a loud, angry curse by armies of aggrieved mothers and grandmothers. He found that he couldn't die soon enough.

The curse did not spare black folks…least of all Paul Robeson. The Nixon Commission never hung the Black Panther thing on him, but in hounding him through travel restrictions, blacklisting, surveillance, and appearances before the House Un-American Activities Committee the US drove him into alternating states of paranoia and depression and ever deeper into the arms of the Soviet Union, a brutal totalitarian state he perceived through rose-colored glasses as a better new deal for African-Americans. In short, he suffered the curse of all bright, talented, prideful blacks of an activist bent in pre-Muhammad Ali America.

In post-Ali America, Kareem X didn't fare much better. Kareem was the son of Marcus Barber by his first wife. Like his hero Malcolm X, Kareem, born Jackie Barber, dropped what he called his slave name and embraced Malcolm's more aggressive approach to achieving racial equality, which ironically would be articulated by Killmonger's father in Black Panther this way: "Their leaders have been assassinated. Communities flooded with drugs and weapons. They are overly policed and incarcerated. All over the planet, our people suffer because they don't have the tools to fight back." Kareem X actually got to hear those lines spoken in 2018 when his three precious grandchildren took him to see *Black Panther* at the local Imax. But Kareem, who always resented his father for falling in love with Milo's mom, a white woman, and befriending Shep, a white man, lost his patience with the film when T'Challa enlisted Ross, the white CIA agent, in helping the Wakandans against Killmonger's coup. Kareem stood up in the theater, raised a clenched fist and screamed at the screen: "Don't trust that motherfucker! Don't trust that white devil! You don't need his help. Don't take it! Damn the white devils. Damn them straight to hell." Kareem's grandchildren hurried him out to the theater lobby where they sympathetically gathered around him. He looked around into their loving, caring eyes and saw reflected back their collective conviction that he had totally lost his mind. The curse sometimes struck with a subtle touch.

Not so, for Milo. Following his reinstatement after shooting to death his mother and Marcus Barber, he rapidly went from being the freshest face on the Enfield police force to its oldest, most bitter. Others were promoted over him or went on to better paying, less stressful jobs elsewhere or were busted on corruption charges for taking bribes that no one ever even bothered to offer him. The resentment built up, and one day while patrolling Pearl, the street where he grew up, he came upon two young dark-skinned boys. They could've been Puerto Ricans; they could've been black kids up from New York; hell, they could've been 4th generation Sicilians whose days in the American sun had failed to bleach out their genetic swarthiness. Milo didn't much care. What he cared about was that they were strolling past the door of the corner shop where he and his buddies used to stop for soda pop after church, past the telephone pole where his old man had fatally wrapped his car after an all-night bender...past the funeral parlor where Sheila, his mom, was solemnly waked while he sobbed uncontrollably at her casket. The young aliens were casually walking over this sacred ground with their pants hanging low and their dusky ass cracks blaspheming the shit all over his world. He stopped and got out of his patrol car and ordered them to pull up their pants. "Fuck you," one of them said. He drew his gun and commanded, "Pull up your damn pants or I'm taking you in for indecent exposure." "Pull up your own pants," the other boy yelled back at him. "I can see your fuckin' belly button lookin' over your belt buckle at me. It's indecent." They both laughed, and so Milo shot them. At his trial before a jury of his peers, he retold details of their obscenities, their disobedience, their sacrilege to his mother's memory...and the jury bought it. But as often happens with bigots, one night the hatred ceaselessly prowling around his brain finally found its real target—himself. He picked his service revolver up off his TV tray, aimed it at his right temple, and pulled the trigger while sitting alone watching "The Wire" on HBO. The last words he heard were, "You feelin' me?"

On the night Milo had shot his mom and her black lover Marcus Barber, Shep was so distraught that he was to blame that Rosemary felt compelled to exercise extreme compassion on him. On the drive back to return the tobacco bus in the pre-dawn hours, they pulled over alongside the Jonathan Edwards boulder on Enfield Street. Under the presumably disapproving eyes of Edwards' angry God, they had sexual intercourse for the first time in their pristine relationship. Nine months after Shep died in her arms on Main Street, Rosemary suffered the curse of being a single mom in the

1950s. She endured it, however, and raised Shep Jr. to become one of the foremost film projectionists in the entire country...3-D, Imax, retro cameras from the 30s and 40s...wherever a highly skilled hand was needed to run a film, Shep Jr. was there.

He was also there when his mom was invited back to Enfield for the launch of a civic drive to save and revive the Strand, which had sunk to utter decrepitude after a brief, dark spell as a porn house. Upon her return, Rosemary took Shep on a tour of her old haunting grounds. They passed by the dirty, darkened green-black marble in the lobby through the doors where crowds had once rushed to see *Black Panther*. They stepped over torn carpet, puddles from leaks in the roof, and floors that though always on the sticky side had become outright mucilaginous. They looked over ripped-up red seats, sagging faux velvet curtains and chunks of fallen plaster. Then they made their way to the projection booth, which neither of them had been in since they said goodbye to Enfield when Shep Jr. was just 8-years old. Shep's son cast the flashlight that had accompanied them on their tour over the grimy walls until it lit upon a message crudely written in whitewash. It read: *The present is a dialog between the past and the future. If we turn a def ear to it, we are cursed.—Shep Farrell.*

Rosemary had never ever seen that there before, but knew it was Shep.

Most def.